A Scars ⌐

by

Charlotte 1

Published in United Kingdom

First Published, 05 Apr. 2017

Charlottelathwell@gmail.com

Dedicated to:

Spencer, who scarred my heart with unconditional love. See you at the bridge little man.

Preface

Dr Sienna Turner may be a renowned and respected Criminal Psychologist but she has a self-made steel wall around herself, protecting her from the world and blocking out the past. Her strength and stone hearted stubbornness have enabled her survival for over ten years.

She moves to Highbridge to work alongside her beloved DCI Sloane. With the help of a police sergeant, who has issues of his own, Dr Turner goes on the hunt for a serial killer.

As they embark in a race against time they engage in their own battle of wills. When her walls begin to close in on her she fears what used to be her tools for survival, may now be the cause of her downfall.

Chapter 1

Cassie was late for work, again. She had missed her bus so decided to take a short cut through the park. She was always apprehensive when going through the large open space so early in the morning, but she'd already had two verbal warnings for her punctuality. Cassie needed this job, even if she didn't think it was fair having to start work at seven on a Sunday morning.

She hurried along from the main road towards the industrial estate where she worked. The first half of the park was overgrown scrubland, or as the council had labelled it, a wild life sanctuary. The only thing that sought sanctuary here however, were bike thieves, dumping their stolen rides home and fly tippers. You could still see the track that used to be a footpath, but in the dim light of a cold early morning, it was precarious going.

It was lighter now but only barely. There was a frosty March, dampness in the air and Cassie pulled her coat tight around her neck as she shuddered out of the cold. She couldn't wait for the summer as she detested the bitterness of winter. As she neared the middle of the park she could see the swings up ahead. She felt a bit safer, seeing them in the distance, knowing they were near the security of the packing warehouses where she worked.

The sound of footsteps speeding towards her from behind temporarily froze her to the spot. Walking faster and faster as the footsteps grew closer, she could feel the panic rising from her stomach into her throat. She was about to break into a run in the hope she could make it to the industrial estate in time. Just then the footsteps sped past her.

"Holy fuck!" Cassie screeched breathlessly, reeling from the fear that was now leaving her body. She slowed back down and continued along the path towards the swings.

As she walked she noticed the jogger had stopped. He was looking down at a dark shape on the ground. She could see him stagger back and bend over. *He's throwing up,* she thought nervously. She knew that whatever he had seen was not good and suddenly she didn't want to move.

Forcing herself forward she could see the jogger was now on his phone while waving his arm at Cassie, motioning for her to stay back. Cassie's throat had gone dry and her stomach had started to knot as the adrenaline pumped through her body.

The jogger started to shout at her, "Stop! Don't come any closer."

Fight or flight had kicked in but instead of fleeing Cassie ran towards the jogger. Something inside told her she could not leave this guy to go through whatever it was he had seen alone. Drawing nearer, she became very aware of the acrid smell, stinging her nostrils. She could now see the fear in his eyes. Looking down towards the shape on the ground, she finally saw what had caused him to vomit. Cassie started to scream and as she did she knew she would wish she had listened to the jogger for the rest of her life.

Chapter 2

Slamming her fists against the sheets, Sienna growled in frustration before pulling the pillow from under her, placing it across her head in a bleak attempt to drown out the sound of the screeching voice coming from outside her apartment building. She'd had another restless night having been unable to get work out of her head. Her insomnia was sure to be the death of her, she surmised. The neighbour's domestic was the last thing she needed at six on a Sunday morning.

Sighing deeply finally accepting her last chance of a lie in was lost she got out of bed, tied her long dark curls up loosely into a bun, threw on a claret silk knee length robe and went to the window. She pulled back the blinds and looked down from her top floor apartment. Sienna always insisted on calling it the top floor, she hated the term 'penthouse', believing it was a conceited notion thought up by property developers and the likes to get more money for climbing more stairs.

She saw a slim blond female hammering on the external doors of the building while buzzing frantically on the entry phone.

"Bloody hell it's like being at work." Sienna complained to herself.

Yawning, she shuffled sleepily out from her en-suite bedroom to the open planned room and went to the kitchen area where she began making a pot of coffee. Hovering over the tin of coffee with the spoon deliberating whether or not to put an extra spoonful of coffee into the filter.

Kill or cure she justified as she heaped in another spoonful of the rich smelling roast blend. As she did, she noticed she still had not opened her mail from the previous day. Picking up the different coloured envelopes, she finished making coffee and sat at the breakfast bar sorting through her mail which consisted of the usual invites to apply for credit cards that charge six thousand percent interest, three statements, and a menu from Tang's Chinese takeaway.

"The only useful thing here" she muttered as she popped the menu and the statements in the kitchen drawer and discarded the rest in the kitchen bin. Just as she took her first sip of coffee all hell broke loose outside, only this time it appeared to be coming from the main stairwell.

She secured her robe, tying the belt tightly. How this would protect her, she did not know. She laughed inwardly at the thought of a would-be killer running screaming in the opposite direction because he noticed she had tied her robe up. She picked up her Sunday newspaper from the mat as she opened the door and popped her head round. The commotion grew louder. It was definitely coming from the stairwell and sounded like the slim blonde had managed to get in. *Paperboy, must've let her in on his way out*, Sienna thought as she slipped bare footed out of her door past the lift to the stairwell.

Opening the door to the stairs she heard the conversation much clearer. The slim blonde was still screaming obscenities only now, Sienna could hear the receiver of the abuse. The low tone of the male voice was replying to the tirade.

"I'm sorry but I never led you on, we spent half a night together, that was all".

"You think you can just use me and that's it? You don't even have the fucking decency to reply to a fucking text?" The woman screamed at him in intense anger.

"Look, I don't know how else I can put it, it was a one off. You don't even know me and I never even hinted it would be any more than a one off. I'm sorry if you got the wrong impression."

Sienna recognised the remorseful voice. He lived on the floor below her and coincidently, she had seen him at the station she was now working from.

A sergeant, she remembered. *Sergeant Callum Blake*, that was it. Once she had recognised the voice, Sienna was no longer surprised at what she was hearing.

Well that was just a matter of time, she thought moodily. 'Mr, One Night', seemed to make a habit of bringing home different women for an evening of so called fun, in fact Sienna recalled seeing women doing the walk of shame, on more than one occasion as she came back from her morning runs.

Finally satisfied nobody was being butchered she went back to her apartment to get dressed. She didn't usually run on a Sunday if she wasn't working. Instead she always tried to treat herself to a lie in. However, thanks to the Casanova copper she thought she may as well go.

Not only did she love her morning runs, they were vital to her both physically and emotionally. Running to her was a pivotal part of survival. It helped her to focus and deal with both the scars from her past and the demons that filled her desk every day.

She had worked extremely hard, becoming a proud mother of two children who were now grown up and starting out on their own adventures. Finally, she was a prominent and highly regarded criminal psychologist. Sienna lectured at several universities nationwide and consulted with police on major cases.

She had fought tooth and nail to get where she was, however. She had hit rock bottom several times. Having been brought up to a life of childhood abuse she went into care at the age of nine. She had been through a horrendous marriage and then a final long-term relationship that nearly finished her off, resulting in a breakdown.

Since then she clawed her way back up to the top, and had fought like a wild cat to stay there ever since. Despite the scars her life had cruelly given her, Sienna felt she had finally found a way of life that not only suited her but enabled her to be the best she could be. She was happy in her own skin and would not let anyone threaten that, even if it did mean shutting the world out and depending on nobody.

Selecting some music on her phone she set of out of her apartment and down the stairwell. Thankfully the woman appeared to have left. However, as she ventured down the stairs she saw the cause of all the commotion, leaning over the stairwell bars looking down towards the exit door below.

He looked up as he heard her approach and smiled nervously. Sienna looked at him properly for the first time and tried desperately not to blush. She could see immediately what all those women might have seen in him.

He was about six-foot-tall, muscular, with piercing blue eyes and a smile that she guessed, would get him pretty much anything he wanted.

Well not me, Sienna thought, snapping her eyes away instantly as she went to pass him on the stairs.

"I'm sorry about all the noise." He spoke quietly with a smile that could charm any bird clean out if its tree.

"It is none of my business," Sienna replied flippantly as she passed him.

"However," she continued, more than a little snootily "it amazes me how you cope with stairs with your knuckles dragging like that, it must become painful."

It was too late; her thoughts became spoken words before her brain had had a chance to engage. This happened frequently when she was putting up her barriers. Sarcasm was her first line of defence. Blinking tightly at her own annoyance, she bolted down to the floor below.

"I thought it was none of your business?" He shouted comically down the stairs after her.

She looked up and there it was again, *that bloody smile.*

"I find it difficult to ignore when somebody acts like a caveman in public!" she retorted while raising one eyebrow giving him her trademark harsh look which had been known to intimidate the bravest of men.

Not this one though, he just smiled as if he had just been thrown a challenge and accepted it willingly. She carried on going down the stairs until she reached the bottom. He called something out but Sienna did not hear what it was. She headed out the main door without looking back and just kept running.

Chapter 3

By nine o clock that morning a crowd had gathered at the main entrance to Philpott's Park, which was now closed off to the public by several police officers who were blocking any unauthorised attempt to enter.

An imposing tarpaulin had been erected just before the centre of the park. The area surrounding the tarpaulin had been secured with blue and white tape. Police vehicles were parked randomly around the area. Groups of police and crime scene officers were combing through the large park, working their way in sections from one end to the other. In the back of a police car, the jogger and Cassie were being comforted by two officers, who were trying to learn about the events surrounding their discovery that morning.

Behind the tarpaulin, DCI Terry Sloane and DI Baz Khatri were stood with a crime scene officer. At their feet the charred remains of a female corpse, which had been burned beyond recognition, was being processed before it could be taken away for autopsy.

The burly, stone-faced DCI was massaging his receding hairline. Turning to the young DI he spoke gravely, "What have the two witnesses been able to tell us?"

"Not much to be honest. The girl is hysterical. I've asked for the FME to look at her back at the station. The other one is shaken too, but I think losing his breakfast earlier helped." The DI shrugged before adding, "We'll see what else we can get from them once they've calmed down a bit."

Nodding in agreement the DCI continued "Well I want their statements as soon as their able, I don't want any information forgotten because we've left it too long."

The burnt corpse was now being taken away for autopsy and the two inspectors walked out from the tarpaulin. The DCI looked round him and then at the crowd which was now increasing in number.

"I want that lot spoken to as well. I don't care how long it takes. I want names, addresses the lot. Somebody saw something. Get officers knocking on doors too." He pointed to the row of houses which edged one side of the park behind a row of trees.

"See if anyone was up early, they may have looked out of a window and seen something." He looked up towards the top of the houses as he spoke.

"Yep, already on it Sir."

Without any acknowledgment of the DI's forward thinking, the DCI clapped his hands together, "Right, we've got a lot of work ahead of us, I wanted this done 'n' dusted by the end of the day." He walked off towards his car while shouting over his shoulder, "I'll see you back at the nick, I'm off to phone the Doc."

The DI watched him leave, *Sure sir, I'll just hitch a lift back!* He laughed to himself. DCI Sloane might be a sour old goat at times but he had a deep admiration for the older man who had taught him well.

Walking off towards the crowd to speak to the officers, he couldn't help thinking this was going to take a lot more than a day.

Chapter 4

Callum walked back to his apartment completely fascinated by the mornings events, especially with his encounter with the doc. He had seen her in passing and had sometimes watched her from his window going on her routine runs. He also could not help noticing that she not only a figure that would make any man with eyes in their head turn and stare, but a natural beauty that many women would spend half their monthly income on at salons to try and match.

He'd already heard about her reputation at the station. He'd been told by the DCI she could not only profile better than anyone, but was also more than capable of cutting the hardest of men down to size with one look and a repose of wit that would leave them cringing and running back under their rocks. He had a taste of that this morning but, rather than make him run a mile, she intrigued him. However, he hoped it wouldn't be awkward at work as he knew that their paths were bound to cross on more than one occasion.

He regretted deeply how he had made the blonde feel, especially knowing the Doc had witnessed it. He felt even more ashamed that he couldn't remember the blondes name either. This happened often with Callum. If he was honest he didn't even enjoy the sex *much*. It was just meaningless, anonymous sex. Thinking back, he could honestly say that he didn't think he had ever 'made love' because that would mean loving someone or at least, caring about them deeply. It was just brief company he needed, usually brought on by a boozy night out with the lads.

He often told himself, his colleagues, and friends that he would stop the games and settle down. After all he was forty next year so it was about time. His friends who were mostly settled in relationships would roll their eyes and make the usual comments about not being able to keep it in his pants if his life depended on it.

Deep down Callum was terrified of getting close to anyone. He had seen is parents go through a messy divorce. Then history repeated its ugly self, with the atrocious breakdown of his own marriage, resulting in his son being taken over four thousand miles away. Callum was terrified of going through that again.

He was secretly ashamed of himself for feeling this way. The big tough sergeant, an ex-squaddie who feared nobody was terrified of a woman breaking his heart. He vowed once again he would one day take that leap of faith, but nobody he had met had been worth facing his fears for. However, this didn't stop him feeling bad about how he had made the blonde feel.

What could also be said about Callum by all that knew him however, was that he was honest, reliable, and never knowingly led anyone on and deep down, he had a heart of gold. He just couldn't let himself get close to anyone of the opposite sex. History told him that despite his son who he adored, the only relationship he ever entertained cost him dearly.

Without realising, Callum's mind turned back to the Doc. He had been briefed about her at the station when she first arrived about two months ago.

Doctor Sienna Turner, a Criminal Psychologist and by all accounts, one of the best criminologists in the country. She was already well liked and respected at work. Her expert field, he'd been told was mainly in serious crime and hostage negotiations. While based at Highbridge, with it being one of the main stations in the south of England, she worked nationally, where ever she was needed.

Callum's mind wandered again, trailing off from thinking about her professional reputation, he couldn't get his mind off the way she looked. She certainly wasn't the stereotypical crazy looking, wire haired old professor he had imagined before her arrival. She was small, about five two he supposed, with a slim, hourglass figure. Despite her petite frame there was a self-guarding, inner strength about her that he didn't think he'd seen before. Oh, she intrigued him alright. The feeling both unnerved and excited him. It was an unfamiliar experience for him.

Shaking himself out of his thoughts, he looked at his phone and realised it was getting on for seven. He swigged back the last of his coffee and headed for the shower. He was on duty in an hour and was already running late. Even so, as he was in the shower, he wondered if he would be seeing the doc at work.

Chapter 5

Stepping out of the shower, Sienna felt much better. She had only managed three miles today but it was enough to banish the demons and clear her head ready for the impending day.

It was her day off and she had planned to sort out the boxes from the move which had been crammed in the spare room for the last two months. It was only a small guest room, and Sienna had plans to turn it into an office. That way she could shut of the horrors that often clouded her job from the rest of the apartment. She didn't want Lily or Jack to see that part of her job whenever they came to visit.

Her children made a point of visiting at least twice a month. Sienna, was overjoyed they were both settled. Jack, the youngest at nineteen, was a handsome, bright, happy-go-lucky young man. He was already in love, and planning a future with his girlfriend Stacey. Lilly was, as her grandmother had put it, the spit out of her mother's mouth. She was twenty-two and single. Working with horses, she only had eyes for all things equine. Men in her eyes had to take second place. Many had tried to compete but had literally fallen at the first hurdle. Lilly was as happy as she was beautiful but her stubborn streak, which she inherited from Sienna ran through her like a stick of rock.

Sienna had Lilly when she was only sixteen and married the father who was her first boyfriend from school. It was far from a happy marriage and had ended badly.

Sienna's mobile rang, vibrating off the coffee table onto the floor breaking her from her thoughts.

"Doctor Turner" She announced in a formal tone as she answered the phone. She only used her title of Doctor when answering her phone to work, or other formalities.

"Hi Doc, it's Terry. Sorry to call you on your day off but could you come in?"

DCI Terry Sloane, as gruff as he appeared, was big on respecting down time so, Sienna knew immediately it was not going to be good news.

"What's happened Terry?" Sienna enquired, as she walked to the kitchen.

"We've got a body at Philpott's Park. Two witnesses found it but they're so badly shaken up we can't get much out of them. Can you speak with them, see what you can do? Also, if you can have a look at the crime scene etcetera, I'd appreciate it". The DCI was sounding strained.

"Do you have any idea who it is?" Sienna queried, referring to the body.

"The body had been set on fire, it's so badly burned. We don't know any more other than it's a female at this stage". The DCI confirmed solemnly.

"Give me half an hour and I'll be there. Are the witnesses at the station? I'll speak with them first, then could you arrange for an officer to take me out to the crime scene?"

DCI Sloane agreed, and having confirmed details, they ended the call and Sienna headed off to get dressed.

While going over the telephone conversation in her mind, Sienna got dressed into a black tailored trouser suit, coupled with a turquoise blouse which buttoned up, showing the slightest hint of cleavage. She worked her thick curls back into a tight bun and applied mascara, and eyeliner, before finishing the look off with a thin dusting of powdered foundation. She hated heavy make-up, begrudgingly wearing what little she did, because at thirty-eight, she felt she needed it more, even though she had received many comments about looking at least five years younger than her actual age.

Sienna quickly assessed herself in the mirror, decided she would have to do, grabbed her keys, phone, and bag then headed out the door.

Chapter 6

Walking into Highbridge station heading up to CID, she was met on the stairs by DCI Sloane.

The DCI was a rugged looking man in his early fifties, with pale blue eyes and grey thinning hair. He spoke with a gruff tone but was respected as being harsh but fair. Sienna had known him for years having worked with him on many occasion as she rose through the ranks of her career. He had a soft spot for Sienna, and the feeling was mutual. In fact, it was the DCI who had encouraged her to make the move to Highbridge. He viewed her as a surrogate daughter, and Sienna looked up to him with her own dad being an out and out monster, she could always turn to him for fatherly advice. He was one of the few people she could trust.

"Doc, thanks for coming so quickly, sorry to skip the pleasantries but we're hitting the ground running with this for obvious reasons."

Handing her a manila file he continued, "Here's what we have so far, we finally managed to get a statement from the male witness. He was first at the scene but the second witness has been in a right state. We've put her in the soft interview room. I need her to corroborate the first witnesses statement."

"I'll see what I can do." She promised, keen to get to work.

"Are you ok to speak to her now? Sergeant Blake is with her. I've asked him to take you out to the crime scene afterwards."

Sienna's stomach lurched at the mention of the Sergeant's name. She slightly regretted her sarcastic comments to him this morning and wished, not for the first time, that she'd stayed in bed.

"I've given you a copy of the crime scene photos but are you sure you're ok to see them?" he asked protectively. "They're pretty grim I'm afraid". DCI Sloane's words interrupted her thoughts, snapping her back into focus.

"Yes, of course. I can't do my job properly without them as you know."

She loathed being cossetted by anyone, but due to her fondness and respect for the DCI she often overlooked it where he was concerned. "Comes with the territory." She smiled.

The soft interview room was thoughtfully designed to look like a lounge. The walls were painted in a neutral fawn and there were framed pictures of woodlands and seascapes on the walls. A comfortable two-seater sofa and two matching armchairs dominated the room arranged around a coffee table. There was a toy area in the corner, consisting of a selection of toys to suit both boys, and girls of various ages. The room looked, and felt warm, and cosy. If it wasn't for the sounds of the busy police officers, coming from outside the room, it could be easy to forget you were sitting in a police station.

A young girl of about nineteen with light brown long hair sat on the sofa with her back to the door. Sergeant Blake was opposite in one of the chairs. He was leaning forwards slightly talking with the girl. A female PC sat in the other chair. As Sienna entered the room, Sergeant Blake straightened and smiled at her. He spoke quietly to the girl, telling her he would be back in a minute but would be right outside the door. Sergeant Blake opened the door and motioned gently for Sienna to step out of the room with him. Turning towards her as he closed the door behind them, he smiled warmly as he spoke.

"Dr Turner, we haven't been formerly introduced, I'm Sergeant Callum Blake, but just Callum is fine".

He held out his hand and Sienna shook it firmly, looking him directly in his deep blue eyes. He was strikingly handsome and she had to secretly shake herself to avert her gaze.

"I prefer Doc, or Sienna thank you." Realising her own haughty tone, she softened slightly, "I only use Doctor if I'm providing evidence in court or signing cheques for my accountant." She stated airily. She would have preferred to keep him in the place she had put him in this morning, but it was more important they worked together professionally right now.

"Okay, Doc." Callum approved, smiling broadly.

"What can you tell me about the witness? How is she doing?" She questioned, steering the conversation back to the task at hand.

"Cassie Masters, twenty years old, the second to see the body. She was on her way to work on the other side of the park and decided to take a short cut. She's a bit calmer than she was but I still haven't been able to get anything out of her. She just keeps talking about the smell."

Callum's face dropped as he continued. "Poor girl. I think it'll be stuck with her for a long time to come. I've contacted her parents and her dad is on his way. I thought she could use the extra support."

Sienna couldn't help but feel touched by his concern for the young girl. "Thank you, I'm sure that will help. I'll do my best to assist but if you could refrain from interrupting while I speak with her. Once I've finished you can ask any questions you like. For me to succeed in getting her to provide you with a worthwhile statement, I need her focus to on me and what I'm saying." Sienna made a point of saying this firmly.

Callum indicated his understanding and opened the door for her, following her into the room. Sienna looked to him and he took this as his queue to introduce her to the witness.

"Cassie, I'd like you to meet Dr Sienna Turner, she's a Criminal Psychologist. If it's ok with you, she would like to talk to you about what happened this morning." Callum sat back in the same seat as before, and Sienna positioned herself on the sofa next to Cassie so she was facing her. Callum couldn't help but smile, when she kicked off her shoes, drawing her knees up on the sofa as if she were in her own front room.

"Hi, Cassie, as Sergeant Blake explained, my name is Sienna. Is there anything we can get you, a cup of tea perhaps?"

"No thank you, I don't think I could keep it down." She looked at Sienna through puffy tear soaked eyes and started to sob again.

Sienna leant forward taking the distraught young woman in her arms, comforting her until she stopped crying. Callum leant over with a box of tissues. Nodding her thanks, Sienna took two or three tissues from the box and proceeded to mop the tears from Cassie's eyes. In order for Cassie to calm down Sienna needed to change the subject for a little while.

Noticing Cassie had beautifully manicured nails she began, "Your nails are amazing Cassie. Do you mind telling me where you got them done? I have been promising myself a decent manicure for months. I'm quite new to this area so I have no idea where to go."

Cassie's focus shifted to her nails, "I do them myself, they take ages but I enjoy doing them."

"Well you're very good! Is that what you do for a living? Perhaps I could get you to do mine."

"No, I work at Wholegates just packing boxes but I'm hoping to go to college soon. I could do yours for you if you like" She offered, still sniffing but already looking a little better.

"I think I'll take you up on that Cassie, that's quite a wasted talent you have there. Is that what you are hoping to do at college?"

"Yeah, that or hairdressing, I can't decide." Cassie then thought for a moment, "What's a criminal psychologist?"

"Well, part of my job is to speak with witnesses to help them remember correctly what they have seen. I also build pictures if you like, of the victims, and in turn the suspects. I then give those pictures to the police to help them catch the bad guys." Sienna winked at Cassie as she finished the sentence.

Cassie smiled back and dabbed her eyes. "I'm sorry I haven't been much use to anyone today, I've never seen anything like that," She stalled, looking around the room, "and the smell, I can't get the smell out" she mumbled shakily, trying so hard to keep it together. "I've probably lost my job too, I'm already on a warning. Sorry was that selfish?"

Cassie was rambling and Sienna could see she was starting to panic again, so reassured her. "Cassie, you have been amazing so far. As for your job, I'm sure Sergeant Blake can talk to with your employer and smooth things over for you. He can be quite a charmer when he needs to be."

She couldn't resist the end of her statement. She saw Callum smile sarcastically out of the corner of her eye as Cassie giggled at her last comment.

"Thank you." She stammered while she took in a sharp inward weep, "That would be great if you could Sergeant, I really need that job" she continued.

Callum agreed, smiling warmly, "Leave it with me Cassie."

Sienna's heart went out to the girl. She could see that she was trying to make a go of her life. "I promise we'll do everything we can to help." Sienna soothed reassuringly.

Cassie thanked her and smiled. She was much calmer now so Sienna felt ready to push forward with the interview. "Now Cassie, if it's ok I'd like to walk you through what happened this morning. Now don't worry, we won't be talking about the body you found." She reassured her before continuing. "When we are focused on something, especially if it's terrifying or traumatic, we don't register what's going on around us. I want to help you remember what was going on around the park, the sounds, the smells, anything unusual.".

Sienna made sure, Cassie understood, and was happy to continue. "We can stop at any time, and take as many breaks as you need. Some people find it helpful to close their eyes, but you can do whatever makes you comfortable. Is that ok with you?"

Cassie sighed, nodding in agreement. Holding both Cassie's hands in hers, Sienna continued. "Now, I'd like you to cast your mind back to what you did first thing this morning. First you got out of bed, what did you do next?"

Cassie explained her routine that morning as Sienna guided her through it step by step. Asking what the air smelt like as she walked into the park, what the temperature was like. Eventually she reached the point when she realised the jogger was being sick. Sienna could see the panic starting to rise again. "It's ok Cassie, cast your mind away from the jogger, did you notice anyone else in the park?"

"No, there was no one". Cassie answered.

"Think about what was around you. Were there any cars parked near the park?"

"No, there..."

"...wait there was a car past the swings, near my work. I remember seeing it because it was behind the building, and not in the car park."

"That's great Cassie, you're doing really well. Now, can you remember what type of car it was?"

"It was old, like an old Golf. My brothers got one in our drive. He was going to do it up, but it's a heap. My dad reckons he's going to get it scraped."

"So it was just like your brother's car." Sienna confirmed.

"Yeah, I think, but I was too far away. I couldn't say for sure, sorry."

"No, that's fine Cassie, that's a great help. Can you remember the colour?"

"Yeah, it was red, definitely red." She reported.

"That's great Cassie, the police can check if there are any CCTV cameras at the back of the building."

Sienna and Cassie continued through the exercise, confirming smaller details. Eventually Sienna knew that she wasn't going to get much more information from Cassie, so she decided to wrap up the interview.

"Cassie, you have done so well. Now if it's ok, I'm going to refer you to a counsellor. You're probably going to need a little bit of help processing what you've been through. In the meantime, I'll give you my card and if you need to talk about anything, I want you to call me anytime ok?"

Cassie took the card and hugged Sienna, thanking her for being so kind adding she could do her nails anytime. Sienna informed Cassie she was going to let the female PC finish with the interview, take a formal statement then, as soon as her father had arrived he could take her home. She reassured the young woman Sergeant Blake would speak to her employer.

Chapter 7

Callum was suitably impressed with Sienna. She had quickly managed to calm the young witness and got her to focus with ease. He was also impressed with Sienna herself. She had brains, strength, and beauty. She scared him witless but excited him at the same time. Not for the first time, he shook himself back to the investigation.

They did not speak as they walked up the stairs to the investigation team until Callum broke the awkward silence. "Doc, about this morning. I'm sorry you had to witness that but it's not how it seemed."

Sienna stopped and turned to face him "Oh, I see, so you *don't* think it's ok to treat women like that", she replied sarcastically.

"I'm not the ogre you think I am, or should I say caveman." Callum argued with a smile.

That smile, Sienna thought. "Well if the sabre-toothed tiger skin fits, Sergeant Blake."

Laughing, Callum matched her sarcasm "Well, you don't need our witness to give you a manicure, I see your claws are already sharp enough."

Sienna, who hated to be beat at anything retorted, "Sergeant Blake, what you get up to in your spare time is none of my concern. However, if you don't want women to call you after you have had your way with them, I suggest you don't give them your telephone number. Also, if you could see your way clear to sleeping with them in their beds and not yours in future, maybe I would not have my very rare Sunday morning off disturbed by hordes of scorned women."

Sienna walked off through the doors of CID, leaving Callum well and truly in his place.

"She's got the measure of you, Cal." Callum turned to see DCI Sloane behind him, laughing.

"Yeah, I don't think we got off to a great start, Sir." Callum laughed, only inside he wasn't laughing at all. For some reason, what the Doc thought mattered to him. It was a new experience and he wasn't sure how he felt about it.

"Bit of advice Cal, I've known the Doc for over ten years. She doesn't suffer fools well. You try and feed her bullshit, you'll end up covered in your own crap."

With that, DCI Sloane patted Callum on the shoulder, and as he walked through to CID he shouted over his shoulder, "You can get some practice when you take her to the crime scene after you've updated me on the second witness."

Callum digested what the DCI advised as he followed him.

Chapter 8

On the way to the crime scene Sienna focused herself on the contents of the manila folder DCI Sloane had given to her earlier. She flicked through a copy of the first witness statement and studied the crime scene photos. Studying the charred corpse, she swallowed to push the bile back down to her stomach. She had seen so many gruesome crime scene photos in her time. Viewing both pictures and actual corpses, which were sometimes severely mutilated, was unfortunately par for the course. However, she still got that same sickening feeling when saw the horrific images. She told herself it was what kept her human. The day it stopped bothering her would be the day she questioned her own sanity.

As Sienna looked at each photo in turn, she spoke for the first time. "Well at least the victim was dead before she was set on fire."

"How so?" Callum enquired.

"She's been arranged in a crucifix position. If you were set on fire you would have been writhing in agony, not lying in the same position hoping the fire would go out."

Interested in Sienna's thoughts, Callum ignored her sarcastic tone and asked, "So, what do you think Doc, a religious nutter"?

"Either that or he's doing it for effect, demanding we look at him and appreciate how great he is." Sienna was feeling nauseous now. "Have either the cause or time of death been confirmed yet?"

"Not as far as I know but the DCI will be chasing that up this afternoon." Callum acknowledged. He glanced across at Sienna to see her searching through her bag. "Lost something?"

Wouldn't surprise me if she's got a can of pepper spray and nunchucks in there to fend off admirers, he thought trying not to laugh out loud.

"My pen, I left home in a rush, I must have left it there." she replied frustratingly.

Callum, spotted a newsagent on the left, and pulled over outside the shop. "Back in a sec."

Probably picking up his subscription of Zoo, Sienna thought scornfully.

Callum exited the shop and made his way back to the car with a grin on his face. He had something in his hand but Sienna couldn't make out what it was. He got in the car, turned to Sienna, and held out a long thin, pink pen covered in silver stars, complete with pink and purple feathers which had been attached to the pen by a small spring. She looked in disbelief from the pen to Callum, who just sat there grinning at her like a ten-year-old schoolboy.

My god, it that really how he sees me? Thought Sienna and was about to ask him what the hell she was supposed to do with the girly offering, when Callum produced a plain black biro. "Just kidding." He laughed childishly.

Sienna was set to complain, "You really are a child aren't you." She could not help laughing as she spoke.

"Please Doc, there's no need for thanks." Callum grinned.

"Sergeant Blake?"

"Yeah?"

"Thanks for the distraction." She spoke more seriously now, but still smiling.

"My pleasure Doc." He thought for a moment, watching her out of the corner of his eye, "So, can we call a truce now?"

"For now!" She agreed unconvincingly, averting her gaze towards the road ahead.

Phillpotts Park was still closed off. There were two officers at the main entrance to the park and another two further back where the scene had been taped off from the rest of the park. Members of the public were still milling about in small groups, gossiping, and pointing to various parts of the park, trying to work out between themselves what had happened, who they supposed the victim was, and who the suspect might be.

As Callum pulled the car into the park, the two officers ushered the bystanders out of the way and waved the car through. The ground, was still wet from both the rain the night before and the morning's mist. He parked the car, turned off the ignition, then looked down at Sienna's feet.

"What?" Sienna snapped, abruptly.

"Just checking you don't have high heels on." He remarked, more than a little condescendingly.

"Oh! Well, why wouldn't I?" Sienna barked. "Nothing I like better than trotting round a muddy field in stilettoes. Wearing suitable footwear would require common sense after all."

Making inverted comma signs with her fingers she added "That's far too much for the 'little woman's' brain to cope with."

"Are you always so bloody defensive?" Callum taunted in mock annoyance.

"Only when I need to be. I can't help it, it's an allergic reaction to idiots." Sienna retorted as she got out of the car.

Sienna headed to the spot where the body had been found, leaving Callum trailing behind. *Shit, this woman is hard work*

Callum thought, smirking as he sped up to match her pace. *For a little woman she can really move when angered.*

Reaching the spot of scorched earth, which was still screened off from the rest of the park with the tarpaulin, Sienna noticed the nauseating smell that still clung to the damp air. She recalled what Cassie had said about not being able to get the smell out from her nose and felt for her again. *That's going to haunt her for some time to come,* she thought sadly, and reminded herself to push Cassie's referral through to the counsellor.

The next thing Sienna noted, was where the body had been displayed. Placed where one naturally made footpath crossed with another. She opened the manila folder again and looked at the photos.

"Did you see the body when it was here?"

"Yep, I was the FOA." He confirmed, interested, again.

"What way was the body facing?"

Callum recalled the body's position was laying with the feet towards the crossroads. They walked out from behind the screen and Sienna stood for a time, occasionally turning to different areas of the park. After a while she told Callum she had seen enough.

Callum lifted the tape for Sienna and she bent slightly to step under it. Straightening, she lost her footing on the wet ground. Callum caught hold of her, pulling her in close as he saved her from falling. In the briefest of moments, their eyes met, Callum could smell the lightly scented perfume Sienna was wearing. His stomach flipped as he peered into her deep brown eyes. *God your beautiful,* he thought. As if reading his mind, Sienna pulled away awkwardly. "We should get back, I need to start on a preliminary profile." she urged, trying hard not to sound flustered.

They walked back to the car in silence and headed back to the station. Neither of them knowing what to make of the short but significant moment of contact.

Chapter 9

Arriving back at Highbridge, Sienna went off to her office and Callum went straight up to CID where he was informed the initial forensic report was back.

The victim had one deep five-inch knife wound and sixteen, three-inch deep lacerations, each one as precise as the next. The victim, finally, had her throat cut open before being moved post-mortem to the park. There was no definitive age yet, but she was estimated to be in her late-twenties. The forensic examiner estimated the victim was killed between midnight and three am.

Aside from the report, two officers had been to the industrial estate where Cassie had remembered seeing the red Golf type vehicle. There was no CCTV at the back of the building where the car would have been parked. However, CCTV at the entrance captured a VW Golf entering the estate at four-sixteen in the morning. Unfortunately, the colour or registration could not be confirmed.

Callum was standing with the investigation team who were discussing the recent updates when a young PC's voice came through on Callum's radio. The PC was breathless from nervous excitement as he reported a possible serious crime. Relaying the address, he requested assistance and scene of crime officers. Callum rushed in to the DCI's office to update him.

"Right, Baz and I will get over there now. Cal, can you update Doc on the pathology report? If this missing woman looks like she could be the victim Doc may want to look at the scene."

"No problem, sir." Callum confirmed and made his way down to Sienna.

At the property, PC Dale Andrews was at the front door and other officers had already arrived. The house was being taped off across the drive and the officers were speaking to neighbours and bystanders. DCI Sloane stood with PC Andrews, who informed him a young woman was reported missing at lunchtime when she didn't arrive at her mother's house. Her mother was concerned because the missing woman was also her main carer and was extremely reliable.

PC Andrews and PC Markowska were called to the property but received no reply. However, they became suspicious when they could hear music coming from inside. They walked around to the rear of the house, looked through the kitchen window and it looked like all hell had broken loose.

In the small kitchen, a nauseating, metallic smell clouded the dry air of the room. Blood which covered the walls and cupboards. A pool of blood and small slivers of flesh covered much of the floor. There was broken crockery everywhere and a stool from the breakfast bar lay on its side. The rest of the property appeared untouched. The woman's purse and car keys sat on a hallway table. On closer inspection nothing appeared to have been taken. The drivers licence in the purse confirmed the woman's name was Elaine Jackson. She was twenty-eight years old. The officers who had spoken with her neighbours confirmed Elaine lived alone.

DCI Sloane asked DI Khatri to go with PC Markowska to the mother's house to update her as much as possible and try to obtain as much information about Elaine Jackson as they could.

Although it would need to be confirmed, the DCI considered all that he had seen and already knew in his own mind the body discovered this morning was Elaine Jackson.

Chapter 10

Sienna wasn't in her office when Callum got there. He felt a pang of disappointment before telling himself to get a grip. He could smell the sweet, floral aroma of Sienna's perfume, which made his stomach flutter as he inhaled. Walking over to her desk, he picked up a small framed photo of a pretty, young woman in her twenties next to a younger handsome man. Both looked very similar to Sienna. Smiling, he placed the photo down gently. He picked up a pen, wrote on the stack of post-its' on the desk, and left. Once again, he felt disappointment that she wasn't there. *What is it about this woman?* He wondered, not for the first time.

Sienna had just come back from her car. Her mobile was dying so she needed her charger. Walking back in to her office she picked up the post-it.

Doc,
Have path report and DCI called out to possible vics house.
Meet   me   in   my   office.
Cal
PS. Please...

She sighed loudly in frustration then went along the corridor to the sergeants' office which was empty. Inside two vacant desks faced each other. There were several filing cabinets and a whiteboard on the wall. She went in and walked slowly around the room. Standing with her back to the door, she wasn't sure whether to wait or not.

"Hey!" The familiar low, deep voice made her jump.

She spun round to see Callum leaning casually up against the door smiling teasingly at her. Sienna's stomach filled with butterflies and she felt her face redden. She felt like a rabbit caught in the headlights but she forced herself to continue. With one eyebrow raised while holding up the post-it, she asked with a disinterested tone, "You wrote?"

Callum smirked, nodding his head towards the note, "Our first love letter." he teased.

"I'll treasure it." Sienna replied sardonically, making sure her barriers were well and truly up.

The sarcasm in her voice was not lost on Callum. Still smiling he walked slowly towards her. When he was close, he leaned in towards her. Sienna held her breath not knowing what to expect. He leaned in closer, before reaching past her, picking up a folder on the desk behind her. He straightened, handing her the file while still standing close.

"One pathology report." He was looking directly into her eyes, teasing her with his smile, knowing that she was flustered.

Daring herself to take a breath, Sienna stepped back. Feeling annoyed at his actions she tossed the file on the desk. "You really do have an over-estimated sense of self-importance, don't you? What is it they say? If I wanted to kill myself I'd jump off your ego."

Stunned at Sienna's retort, Callum stood speechless before finally biting back. "That's rich coming from the ice queen." He laughed.

"Actually, I'm usually a nice person, so if I'm cold towards you, it says more about you than it does me." She replied, conceitedly.

Her airy tone made Callum realise he wasn't going to win, so he backed off, holding his hands up in surrender. "Okay wildcat, you've won this battle but the war's not over yet." He winked at her as he finished speaking, firing his final shot before retreating to his desk.

"Oh please, you don't have the mental capacity to take me on, and as I pointed out before, it's Doc or Sienna *not* ice queen, wildcat or any other pet name you label women with."

She snapped up the file and made her way to the other desk. She sat down and turned her focus back to the investigation.

Callum sat at his desk, watching her in disbelief. Oh, she was a piece of work alright. Rather than put off however, Callum felt the exhilaration soaring through him like a bolt of lightning.

Chapter 11

It had been 48 hours since the jogger and Cassie had found the charred remains, in Philpott's Park. The time had flown by. Evidence was still being collected but it was confirmed from dental records the body was Elaine Jackson. DNA was still pending. However, this was now just a formality.

The victim's mother had been informed and the DCI had made a statement to the press appealing for witnesses and asking the press to respect the family's privacy at this sad time. The station was buzzing, and the briefing room was now a major incident room.

Sienna was in with the DCI talking about the case. She had asked for the family liaison officer to speak to the victim's mother to arrange for her to visit. The DCI agreed, promising he would get on to it in the morning. Sienna agreed.

"So how soon can you have a profile together Doc?"

"Now I have all the reports in, with the exception of the mother, I can hopefully have an initial report for you by tomorrow." Sienna replied. "I'd like to visit the victims house too if somebody can escort me out there." As she spoke she wondered if Sergeant Blake would be that somebody.

"Sure, I'll get someone to run you out there when you're ready." The DCI then thought some more.

"If it's ok with you, I'd like Sergeant Blake to work with you on this case."

Did he just read my mind? Thought Sienna nervously.

"Thanks for coming in on Sunday Doc. I know you was looking forward to the rest. I hope we didn't mess up your plans too much."

"Nothing that can't wait, besides, the morning was already ruined all thanks to the apartment buildings resident lothario."

The DCI looked at her curiously "Tell me more."

Sienna re-laid Sunday's events on the stairwell to the now amused DCI.

"Cal's not as bad as you think, Doc. He's got a heart of gold in there somewhere. He's just a nightmare when it comes to relationships, as in he doesn't do them." He went on further.

"He's just a coward when it comes to the thought of settling down. He got well and truly shafted by his ex while he was in the army. He left there to try and save his marriage but it was too late. She took his kid and ran off to America with another bloke."

Sienna was listening intently as the DCI continued.

"It really fucked him up for a long time. Apparently, his dad was an arsehole too which never helped. I reckon he just needs to meet the right woman." As spoke, his eyes narrowed as he looked at Sienna.

"Okay, you can stop that right now Terry." She bit, laughing out loud. "I know that look and I'm not going there. You're always trying to set me up with someone. What is it with you? Do you want to buy a new hat or something?" She added still laughing.

"You can't blame an old man for trying." He joked.

"Well you tried and you failed. Now give it up."

Shortly after, Sienna hugged her surrogate father and left to get on with her profile.

Chapter 12

Sienna's office was a small but sufficient room on the ground floor, just off from the custody suite and sergeant's offices. With it being set further back from all the hustle and bustle of the main part of the station, she enjoyed the peace and quiet it offered her. She sat at her desk going through notes and compiling her report to present to the investigation team. All the photos and reports on the case were splayed out on her desk. Her mind was in full flow as she focused on all the information laid out before her. Writing at speed, stopping occasionally to pick up a photo or re-read different parts of the reports. She always wrote by hand, only using her computer to type the final draft. She found from experience, her mind worked better this way.

Once she had finished writing she went through the report again, circling different sentences, or phrases, crossing out or inserting other words throughout the document. She then read it again before typing the report out. Proof reading it for a final time while making any corrections, Sienna was finally satisfied. She saved the document and printed off enough copies to pass round the team. She gathered up all the photos and reports, placing a copy of her report on top of the pile, then put it in the manila folder. Finally ready to give her initial profile, Sienna headed up the stairs to the briefing room.

The large, noisy room was well lit with windows covering the width of the left wall. A large table sat centre of the room with chairs arranged messily around it. A projector sat on the table facing front, there were several files, and note books placed next to it, ready to be handed out. Half-drunk plastic coffee cups which left a faint smell of stale, cold coffee were scattered over the table. To the front of the room there were two large white boards covered in writing and mind maps of various colours. There was a screen which was covered with photos of the victim's remains and the two crime scenes. To the left hung a large map of the area surrounding Philpott's Park. To the right there were two smaller empty desks.

On the right wall there were three posters. One was about information governance and another was advertising the annual charity ball which raised money each year for the chosen charity of the moment. This year, she noted for the UK Victim Support Network. The final poster was about equality in the work place, depicting several officers of differing gender and race.

There were about fifteen officers of varying ranks in the briefing room. They stood in small groups talking amongst each other. DCI Sloane was standing with DI Khatri. On the other side of the room, Callum was standing with another Sergeant, who Sienna recognised as Dave Fletcher. He was a thin, dark haired man, who she guessed was in his mid-forties. She had spoken to him on several occasions and found him to be a warm, friendly man with a wickedly, funny sense of humour. In the conversations Sienna had with him, she had already worked out that he only had two loves outside the job, his family consisting of his wife and two daughters and his motorbike.

The DCI acknowledged Sienna as she entered the room, and after a few minutes he called for silence.

"Right," He called for attention, clapping his hands together, "we've got a lot to get through so if you could all listen up."

Sienna perched herself on a nearby table at the front of the room facing the others. She had to tiptoe in order to lift herself on to the table. This did not go unnoticed by Callum who chuckled at the sight. In turn, his laughing at her did not go unnoticed by Sienna who smiled at him scathingly. Dave Fletcher caught the cynical look and laughed out loud, "Fuck me Cal, if looks could kill, I'd be on you with the defib shouting clear by now."

Callum laughed with him. "She hates me mate, we got off to a bad start and it went downhill from there."

"Mate, that ain't hate trust me. Last time my missus looked at me like that, we had our second kid nine months later."

Before Callum could reply the DCI roared for quiet again.

When the room fell silent, the DCI continued, "Okay, so let's start from the beginning."

"At seven sixteen this morning, Sergeant Blake and PC Ainsworth attended a report of a body at Philpott's Park. On arrival they discovered the remains of a body which had been set on fire. We now know this body to be Elaine Jackson…"

The DCI then went on to describe, in detail, witness information, details of the vehicle spotted by Cassie Masters, and the subsequent CCTV footage. When he had finished he moved to the details surrounding the scene of the murder and the events surrounding it.

"…PC's Andrews and Markowska were called to 52 Larkin Road earlier today following the report of a misper."

The DCI slowly paced the floor as he spoke, "The state of the property and subsequent DNA, confirms this is where Elaine Jackson was murdered."

He stopped and faced the room. Slowing his voice he went on, "The pathology report confirms the Elaine Jackson was stabbed 17 times before her throat was cut."

"She was then taken to Philpott's Park, covered in petrol and set on fire."

"Unfortunately, we're unable to tell if she had been sexually assaulted, due to the level of damage to the body." He looked around the room as if to highlight the severity of the crime, if at all it needed highlighting.

The DCI proceeded give the estimated time of death and forensics thoughts on the murder weapon which they believed to be a short, thin blade. He then began creating a timeline on one of the white boards where he listed, in chronological order, the last time the victim was seen, when the car was spotted, through to when she was discovered and finally reported missing.

He finished with his briefing, and acknowledged PC Markowska who began handing out files to all the officers in the room.

"Now I'm going to hand you over to Dr Turner who I've asked to consult with us on this case."

Sienna stood up and walked to the centre of the room. She passed the stack of reports that she had copied earlier to the officer nearest to her and asked her to take one and pass the rest round. When she had everyone's attention she began to deliver her initial profile.

"Before I begin I should tell you, this is an ongoing profile. In other words, it will be developed more over the coming days if necessary."

She paused as her eyes darted round the room, making sure everyone understood. She walked to the screen containing the crime scene photos, standing sideways so she could both address the room, and indicate relevant photographs.

"If we look at the body first. The initial stab wound was the deepest, rendering her too weak to move and before her throat was cut, he inflicted a further sixteen wounds which were precisely, three inches deep and arranged in a neat, symmetrical pattern." She pointed to the image on the screen as she spoke, her fingers tracing each wound.

"Both the depth of these wounds and the pattern are significant to him." Sienna paused, wondering about them herself.

PC Andrews interrupted, "Why?"

"Generally, people who kill in this way," She pointed to the photo's again, "are offloading significant trauma. Childhood sexual abuse, or severe neglect for example. Possibly copying an event or events they have witnessed, or even endured themselves."

"So you're telling us this nutter did this because his mummy didn't give him enough cuddles?" PC Andrews grunted with contempt. "Well that's narrowed it down. We'll be here all year looking for him."

Callum was about to address the insolent junior officer but Sienna beat him to it.

"How do you know there are so many to question PC Andrews? Are you one of them?" She countered.

The officers in the room began to laugh.

"Funny!" He retorted, angry that she had embarrassed him.

"Sit down PC Andrews." Callum called out firmly, "unless you have anything worthwhile to contribute keep your mouth shut."

Sergeant Dave Fletcher who always had a way with words looked towards Sienna, "Carry on Doc, ignore PC Andrews over here, he still ain't got over the fact he'll never be the man his mother is."

Everyone in the room roared with laughter, except Sienna, who was trying her hardest not to, and of course, PC Andrews."

"Right come on you lot." The DCI Bellowed. "We've got a lot to get through and PC Andrews, you ever disrespect a colleague in my earshot again you'll deal with me." He turned to Sienna, "Doc, if you'd like to continue."

"Aside from the message he may be trying to convey," she continued, "The fact the killer has taken the time to be so accurate shows not only, has he fantasised about this for a long time before this kill, but he has practiced before, possibly with animals. It is also entirely possible," she continued, "that he has killed before."

As she pointed this out there was a low murmur throughout the team.

"I would suggest looking at similar unsolved crimes in other areas of the country. Also look for anyone who has been charged with cruelty to animals. This would have been during adolescence." Sienna paused to allow the various officers who were taking notes to catch up.

"Moving on to the position of the body. This was arranged in a crucifix position at the junction of two pathways in the park. He has purposely placed her where she had the most chance of being found. He wanted to create a shock factor."

"This," she emphasised, pointing at the screen, "is his message. He wants us all to sit up, take notice and fear him."

As she spoke her mind wandered back to the depth of the lacerations. Something about them was eating away at her, but she couldn't work out what it was.

"There is also a high chance he returned to the scene when the police and public were there. He could have been in the crowd of onlookers seeking more gratification for the chaos and fear he created."

PC Andrews interrupted again, "Why, would he come back? Surely, he wouldn't risk a capture."

"Firstly, he would not go to the trouble of mutilating and arranging the body in such a fashion, if he could not witness the effect it had on the police and people around him. Even the burning of the body was not so much as to hide forensic evidence but to add to the chaos, to horrify, and spread fear. He would want to see that fear."

"Secondly, with both his arrogance, believing he can't be caught, and drive for the ultimate satisfaction nothing would keep him from returning."

"Next, the report from Elaine Jackson's house states. There was no sign of a break in. He has taken his time to gain the victims trust so she would allow him to enter the property. It takes meticulous planning to find the prey, stalk and finally, kill."

Referring to her notes briefly she added, "I understand you are already speaking to family, neighbours and friends. However, I would also advise gaining access to any social media to see if she met anyone online." She looked towards the DCI, "If you haven't already that is?" She questioned.

"It's a good point, there was a home computer taken to forensics. We'll make sure it's checked."

Sienna went on to describe her thoughts of the killer's personality.

"Your suspect has no conscience, no behavioural limits and he gets extreme pleasure from the cruelty he does to others. He will be manipulative and incapable of speaking the truth. He is intelligent and may have a managerial job. He will appear to the public to be amenable and sociable. This is a mask he uses to disguise his true self. A means to an end if you like. He will have grandiose feelings and may even believe he was put on this earth for a greater purpose."

Nearly finished, she walked back to the centre of the room to face her audience. "Oh, and one more thing," Sienna paused and looked round the room, making sure she had everyone's attention. "He's not done yet, in fact, he is highly likely to keep killing until he's caught." With this final statement there was a stony silence in the room. Sienna could see the seriousness of what lie ahead of the team embedding even deeper.

She spoke again breaking through the quiet. "That's all I have for now, are there any questions?"

Sergeant Fletcher raised his hand, "What makes you think he's killed before?"

"According to the PM report, there was confidence to the injuries. If this was his first time, there would have been hesitation, shallower wounds. Also, rather than the precise, and symmetrical pattern of the wounds there would have been more variation."

Thinking for a brief moment, she added, "I would expect his first kill would show more hesitation to the injuries."

"Why do you *assume* the suspect is a male?" PC Andrews enquired scornfully.

"Murders with this level of violence are for the most part carried out by males. Females who display this level of depravity rare. That's not to say females should be ruled out from your enquiries. In particular, there may even be a submissive female partner who is either scared to speak, or willing to cover for him in order to please him."

Finally, from Callum; "Are you certain he's going to kill again, Doc?"

"I'd stake my career on it." Sienna replied, adamant in her statement. "The excitement, and sexual relief he gets from not only the killing but the displaying of the body, and the carnage he is creating won't let him stop. His desire and drive for gratification, the ultimate high if you like, will become harder and harder to achieve, forcing him to seek even more disturbing thrills."

Callum, was quite impressed with her conviction.

There were no other questions so, Sienna thanked everyone for listening, and went back to the table she had previously been sitting on.

The DCI then gave out instructions to everyone, assigning each officer to a particular task, finally turning to Callum. "Sergeant Blake, I'd like you to work alongside Dr Turner on this case, assisting her wherever she needs it, visiting the family etcetera."

"Yes Sir." His eyes met with Sienna's as he smiled.

"Ok everyone, let's get to work. The sooner we get this sick bastard, the better." He then ordered everyone that had been there since the early hours of the morning to go home and get some rest. "I'll see you back here at eight AM sharp." He instructed.

DCI Sloane walked over to Sienna and thanked her for the profile, then waived Callum over.

"You both need to get home and get some sleep."

Before Sienna could protest he added firmly yet with a fatherly tone, "There's nothing you or Cal can do until tomorrow."

"What about you Terry? You've been here since the early hours."

"Don't worry about me, I'll get my head down here."

"Now go on both of you, home. I need you both focused tomorrow."

Sienna resigned herself to the DCI's orders and both she and Callum headed out.

There was an awkward silence walking downstairs together. They walked through the custody suite and when they reached the sergeant's office, Sienna spoke first.

"Right then, I'll see you in the morning. Eight ok for you? Assuming you're not fighting off angry women that is."

"If it makes you feel any better, I'll barricade my door until morning."

"Going into hiding? Figures!" Sienna countered.

Callum held up his hands and raised his eyes to the ceiling.

"I can't win!" He shouted, as Sienna went to her office.

Chapter 13

Sienna got home just after seven that evening and she was more exhausted than she had let on to the DCI. As she walked up the stairs, Callum was standing in the spot he was in on Sunday morning.

"Are you stalking me now?" Sienna barked.

"Not yet." he replied grinning. He tilted his head to one side and his grin softened.

"Why do you never use the lift?" he asked.

"If you must know, I don't like them."

"Nothing wrong with being scared."

Sienna folded her arms, "I did not say I was scared," she shifted uneasily, leaning from one foot to the other, "I simply don't like them."

"Is it so hard to admit you're scared?" Callum was both amused and curious at her defensiveness.

Sienna rolled her eyes and looking at him, she raised one eyebrow in annoyance, "Look Sergeant Blake, if I was scared then I would say I was scared," Not confident that she had won, she added "Some of us," her eyes narrowed as she unfolded her hands placing them on her hips, "are not afraid to admit our flaws."

Smiling he shook his head and closed his eyes in resignation, "Oh, you're a real piece of work, you know that?" He straightened spoke again, "Come in, have a coffee with me."

"Is that an order or a request?"

"A request." He was now holding the stairway door to his floor open, staring at her intently with his piercing blue eyes.

She was about to object when Callum stopped her by speaking first. "Come on Doc, we're going to be working together, let me prove to you I'm not a knuckle dragging caveman. Just 10 minutes."

"It'll take more than 10 minutes to prove that hypothesis."

"As long as it takes then." He laughed.

"Okay, okay, I'll have a coffee with you, but you've got 5 minutes."

"Deal!" Callum promised, smiling as he waived her through the door.

Callum's apartment, was pretty much the bachelor pad she had expected. It was much the same layout as Sienna's penthouse but, with only one bedroom and no balcony. The apartment was extremely clean and tidy, nearly to the point of obsession. *Army life* she thought as she recalled her conversation with the DCI that afternoon.

The walls were a light slate grey with a black leather three-seater sofa and a glass coffee table with matt black frame sat on top of a monochrome rug. The spicy scent of Callum's aftershave, and the percolating coffee, mixed in the air making a heady fragrance, which simultaneously comforted, and unnerved her. Next to the TV, there was a glass cabinet which matched the coffee table which held pictures of Callum and a young boy, *his son,* she thought. There was also a picture of him and Sergeant Dave Fletcher and one of Callum on his own wearing army uniform. She picked up this last picture, not wanting him to know she had been discussing him with the DCI and she turned to him holding out the picture towards him. "You're ex-army?"

"Yep, for thirteen years from school. I came out at twenty-eight and joined the Met. Milk and sugar?" He asked, while arranging two coffee cups.

Sienna shook her head and walked over toward the kitchen area. She pulled out a stool from the breakfast bar and used the run on the bottom of it to lever herself up onto the seat. Callum noticed out of the corner of his eye and remarked cheekily, "I have a step ladder in the cupboard if it helps."

"Very funny Sergeant Blake, I have never heard a joke about my height before. You must praise yourself daily for your originality." She looked at her watch, "Oh, and you have four minutes left."

"I'm sorry but you just make teasing you so easy." Callum turned to face her, "What are you about five foot two?" He enquired.

"Yes, not that it matters to anybody but you, and how exactly, do I make it easy?"

"You're so fiery and defensive. Scared to let anyone through that steel exterior for fear of them getting to know the real you." He turned back to pick up the steaming mugs of coffee and placed one across the counter in front of her.

"Firstly, this is the real me, like it or not."

"and second?"

"Secondly, you're a fine one to talk about barriers. I suppose you're trying to sleep your way through the female population of London because you're NOT afraid of getting hurt?"

"Well, little miss know-it-all, firstly, I haven't slept with as many women as you think."

"and second?"

"Second, I like the real you." He gave that smile again, and butterflies returned in Sienna's stomach as she blushed.

Refusing to acknowledge the second statement she replied, "Maybe you haven't slept with that many but you treat women like a menu."

"Oh really? Care to explain?" He enquired.

"Once you've sampled one dish you no longer want to eat from that menu again. So, you move on to the next without so much as a tip."

Callum was amused at her analogy "Maybe I just haven't found the right menu yet."

"Oh, I don't think there's a menu in the world that you'd be brave enough to even want to stick with." She countered.

"Well I'm getting more hopeful every day." As he spoke, he stared into her eyes, her pupils were dilated and he had to fight with himself to look away.

Sienna felt the pull of him and she knew if she didn't get out of there, she was going to be in trouble. She looked at her watch again.

"Time's up I'm afraid." She announced, briefly tilting her head slightly to one side.

So am I Callum thought, sad that there five minutes had come to an end. "So soon?" He leant across the counter so he was close to her. She could smell the heady scent of Callum's aftershave.

"So, what's the verdict then Doc? Caveman or just misunderstood?"

"Oh what, five minutes in your company and I'm supposed to melt? Well Sergeant Blake, I'm afraid the jury's still well and truly out." She smiled sarcastically, raising one eyebrow.

Callum knew that he couldn't give up. He was hypnotised by her. The fierceness of her was like a magnet. He wasn't sure exactly what it was he was feeling, but it was heady stuff.

"Come to dinner with me. Just as a friend. If you still think I'm the devil incarnate after that, I promise I won't try to convince you anymore."

"Why does what I think matter to you?" Sienna pulled her head back so she could assess him.

Callum opened his mouth to speak, and closed it again. He couldn't answer because he didn't know why it was so important. As he straightened and looked to the floor, Sienna could see he was struggling and decided to give him a way out.

"I tell you what, if we can make it through tomorrow without me wanting to murder you with your own baton, then I will come to dinner with you." She surrendered.

Relieved that she had let him off the hook he was dangling from precariously, he held out his hand, "You're on!"

Sienna shook his hand and the contact sent volts through them both. She had to go, now. "I really need to go, we have an early start tomorrow."

"Why don't you ride in with me? It makes more sense." Callum suggested, thoughtfully.

For once, Sienna could not see a reason to argue as she slid off the stool and headed for the door. "Ok, I'll see you at seven thirty?"

He opened the door for her and stood close to her. "It's a date!"

Sienna walked out the door towards the stairs "No, Sergeant Blake, it's not."

Chapter 14

Emilie Wythe was in her room with her music blaring. After recently moving down from Manchester to study law at university she didn't know many people yet. She shared a student let with two other girls. They all got on, but her two housemates had their own clique, and Emilie was often left out.

Sitting on her bed with her laptop, she was giggling away while twirling her blonde hair in her fingers. She was in a chat room talking to a young student from another university across the other side of the city. They had been talking for about two weeks and for someone like Emilie, whose anxiety, made it hard for her to meet people, her new online friendship was the perfect answer. Unlike most people her age, going out to meet people in clubs or bars would fill her with dread rather than excite her. She was happy hiding behind the safety of her keyboard.

They had swapped pictures and she was attracted to him. He was warm, friendly, and always complimenting her. He was great for her confidence. Just the tonic she needed.

Recently, he had been asking her to meet him and she had finally agreed. Emilie was actually excited at the prospect of seeing him in person.

Kyle15: Have you told your housemates about us? Xxx

EmilieW: No! Don't think they get it. U know, the meeting online thing Xxx

Kyle15: Maybe they'll understand when we've met. Can say we met at club...

...can't w8 2 meet u. Still on for 8? Xxx

EmilieW: Yep. w8 4 u outside? Xxx

Kyle15: Cool can't w8 xxx

Emilie typed goodnight, and logged out. She went to her wardrobe and began sorting through her clothes, pulling out several different outfits. She wanted to wear something special for their first date. She really wanted him to like her.

She picked out a short skirt, an off the shoulder top, black opaque tights, and boots. She sat back on her bed and looked again at the picture of Kyle on her mobile, tracing his perfectly shaped face with her finger. He was fit and she couldn't wait.

----o----

On the other side of the city just outside Highbridge town centre, a man sat at his computer. On the screen there was a picture of a pretty girl of about eighteen, with long blonde hair and sparkling blue eyes. The man lifted his hand and ran it lightly down the screen. He turned his hand into a fist and clenched it until his knuckles went white. He then moved the mouse and clicked on an icon. A new screen appeared revealing an online chat room.

EmilieW: Yep. w8 4 u outside? Xxx

Kyle15: Cool can't w8 xxx

EmilieW: Night xxx

Kyle15: Xxxx

EmilieW has left the room....

Logging out of the chat room and shutting down the computer, *Oh, I really can't wait Emilie.* He pondered over meeting her, excited at the thought of all they would do together.

Chapter 15

It was six thirty in the morning and Sienna's alarm started blaring out suddenly, causing Sienna to jump before slamming her hand around blindly on the bedside cabinet until she found the alarm's off switch. She lifted her head slightly before dropping it heavily back onto the pillow.

Once again, she hadn't managed to get much sleep. Her thoughts had been filled with disfigured, mutilated bodies. When she finally slept, she dreamt she was being stabbed. In her sleep she could feel each of sixteen incisions being driven through her body as the faceless man loomed over her laughing as he went about his work on her. She woke in the night, soaked with sweat, struggling for her breath. After she lay there for hours, before finally succumbing to sleep.

She rolled over and groaned, putting her hands over her face. Callum would be calling for her in an hour and she felt like hell. She sat up and rubbed the sleep from her eyes. Reaching over, she switched on the light.

There would be no time for a run this morning so she promised herself she would run a couple of extra miles tomorrow. She got up and went out to the kitchen. Making herself a strong pot of coffee before jumping in the shower. By seven she was dressed and sitting at her breakfast bar. Taking her first sip of coffee, there was a knock at the door.

She looked at her watch to double check she wasn't running late and went to the door, knowing who it would be. Callum was in civvies, wearing dark chinos and a light collarless long sleeved top. She inwardly approved as the butterflies in her stomach made themselves known again.

"I thought we agreed seven thirty?" Sienna queried sounding cross. She moved aside to allow Callum through the door.

"Well good morning to you too." Raising his eyebrows as he spoke. "I take it you're not a morning person?" He added as he walked across to the kitchen area, and placed his jacket on the counter.

"I am when I actually sleep." She complained, walking towards   the   percolator.   Coffee?"

"Please." He tilted his head to one side in concern, "Why couldn't you sleep?"

"Hazard of the job." She sighed, as she poured the coffee.

"Is there anything I can help with?" Then, studying her closely, he continued, "You do look tired, still beautiful of course, but tired." Winking as he spoke.

Good save! Sienna thought smiling. She appreciated not only his concern but his attempt at reassuring her that she didn't look a complete wreck.

"I'm fine, but thank you." She placed the coffee in front of him and walked round to his side of the counter. "Apparently sleeping is for amateurs anyway." She laughed.

Callum picked up the coffee gratefully and they sat at the breakfast bar together. He caught the scent of her perfume again. He closed his eyes for a second, savouring the flowery aroma.

"So what's the plan for today, Doc?"

"Victims home first," she picked up her coffee and blew the swirling steam away, "then to visit her mother if that's ok with you."

"No problem." he shrugged, smirking as he sipped his coffee. "Wow I've been here a whole ten minutes and you haven't kicked my arse. There's hope for us yet." He mocked, hiding a cheeky grin behind his coffee cup.

"Don't push your luck." She nudged him as she spoke causing him to lurch forward spilling coffee down his front.

"Oi violent!" He laughed, jumping up before the hot coffee made contact with his skin.

"I'm sorry," She chuckled, "but now you know not to antagonise me first thing in the morning."

"Okay, okay, noted. I surrender!" She threw a tea towel at his chest and he dabbed at the coffee soaked shirt. "I'll need to pop in and change now. See, that's, why I was early."

"Oh, I see, psychic as well as annoying!"

"Well the peace didn't last, long did it?" he jokingly pointed out.

Sienna smiled, then responded mockingly in a motherly tone, "Come on sloppy, let's go and get you changed."

They went down Callum's flat, and he pulled his shirt off over his head as soon as he got in the door. Sienna couldn't help but notice his, well-toned, lightly tanned back. He had a tattoo depicting an eagle with the wings outstretched across his back. The tattoo only helped to highlight his muscular frame. She quietly drew in her breath at the sight. He came back from the bedroom doing up a fresh top, warning Sienna that she would be doing his laundry if there were any more vicious assaults. She told him to shut up as they headed out towards the carpark.

Chapter 16

Frank, and Sam were walking down Hersham Road behind the bin lorry, picking up the scores of black sacks filled with discarded rubbish and foul smelling food as it rotted inside the plastic sacks. Sam, the younger of the two but twice as sure of himself was regaling Frank with his weekend exploits.

"She had a face like one of these," he shouted over to Frank as he held up a ripped bag, allowing rotting potato peelings to spill out over the road. "Had tit's the size of airbags though!"

"Sam, you're a fucking nightmare, surprised you ain't got crabs by now."

"Nah, too careful for that mate." He bragged cockily, kicking the peelings into the gutter.

Armed with several filled bags in each hand, they reached the lorry and tossed the bags in, as the compactor pushed them further into the body of the vehicle. They walked over to the next pile of sacks which had been put there the night before by various residents.

"I didn't stay the night though. Ain't no way I was risking waking up to that." He bent to lift up the first two bags. "I don't mind a quick shag, but I don't do horror stories."

Sam lifted the bags and saw a large object roll from the remaining pile and hit his boot. He looked down and stepped back in horror, shaking his leg as if he had been bitten. A shrill, blood curdling scream emitted from deep within his stomach. Frank jumped back, looking down to see the shape, which had blood soaked, matted hair. The mouth appeared fixed, and contorted into a scream and pale lifeless eyes stared up at him. He pushed Sam back and pulled out his phone, dialling 999. As he did, he couldn't help but notice the dark wet patch, spreading across Sam's crotch.

Chapter 17

Sienna and Callum arrived at Elaine Jackson's house just before eight. The Forensic team had done all they could do the day before so they finally had authorisation to enter the two-story, semi-detached property. A tired looking officer stood at the gate as a group of teenage boys were riding up and down the road on their bikes, trying to get a look inside the property from the road, shouting profanities at the less than amused PC.

Callum told the officer that he would be relieved in half an hour, advising he should go and get some rest. The officer thanked him, as Sienna and Callum walked past to the door of the property.

Sienna was in the front room, looking through a photo album she had found in the wall cabinet. There were photographs of the attractive blonde at various stages of her life from teenage years through to adulthood. Sienna noted that the photographs centred mainly on just a few people who she gathered to be family. There were no social gatherings to speak of. No nights out with friends, captured for prosperity.

"Did they have any luck with the computer?" Sienna asked, without looking round. Callum was looking through a pile of envelopes that were on the dining table at the far end of the lounge. "It's still with forensics but so far they know she had two social media accounts; Facebook and a chatroom." He put down the letters and walked over to Sienna.

Closing the album, she looked up at Callum "Could you chase that up?"

"Sure, I'll get on to it when we get back."

"Looking at her photographs," she handed the album to Callum, "I don't think she had a large circle of friends."

Callum opened the album and started to flick through the stiff pages and agreed, "So, she was a loner."

"What about a mobile phone?"

"There wasn't one." He remarked,

Sienna looked around and walked back out to the hall and came back in. "If she was a carer for her mother, how did she stay in contact with her?" Pointing towards the hall, she added, "There's no landline."

"It definitely wasn't with the body" he recalled. "I'll get someone to check the phone networks."

They looked through the rest of the house, then headed over to Elaine's mother's. Reenie, as she liked to be called was still too distraught to give them much of any use. She did confirm however, that Elaine Jackson did not have any friends to speak of. Her life consisted mainly of working as a receptionist for a small advertising company and caring for her. She told them that she'd always wanted grandchildren but Elaine was always too busy to meet anyone.

They got the name of Elaine's employer and when they said goodbye to Reenie, Callum called through to the investigation team to send someone over to speak with them. Getting through to the team he was about to speak but fell quiet. Sienna noticed and right away the feeling of knowing dread, filled her body. Listening and uttering the odd reply, he hung up the call, and looked at Sienna.

"They've found another one, haven't they?" Sienna asked, with a tightness in her voice.

"She'd been dismembered and dumped on a rubbish collection route." He swallowed before continuing, "The body parts were hidden under different piles of bin bags that were due for collection this morning."

Sienna, closed her eyes tightly. The killer had upped his game, just as she predicted.

Chapter 18

The next three days went with a blur. As details of the second murder reached the news, there was an air of panic in the area of Highbridge.

The DCI had given press statements. Sienna sat alongside him, delivering a profile suitable for public ears to the media. She spoke to them clearly and succinctly, with an air of confidence that made them listen without interruption. Once she had finished she invited the press to ask questions which both her and the DCI answered together. Press photographers, took their fill of pictures for the front pages of the next day's papers, while news cameras filmed them from the side of the room as they spoke.

The DCI finished with the usual warnings of allowing police to do their job, appealing for witnesses, and giving out the crime hotline number.

Inside the station, Sienna provided the team with an update on her profile and advised that the victims more than likely met their killer online. She reiterated the importance of accessing the chatroom that Elaine had been using but the account had been cleared and there was nothing of any significance on the hard drive.

Callum was busy with the inspector and Sergeant Mitchell reorganising rotas to cover the extra shifts needed. Having worked twelve hour shifts over the last week, Sienna decided she needed to clear her head and get some rest. Her focus was clouded from lack of sleep and she couldn't think properly. With Callum, still busy she got taxi home. They had been travelling in together daily as it made more sense for them to car pool.

After viewing the images again of the dismembered body, she felt unclean. Her head was filled with the killer's mind. She wanted a drink but decided it wasn't a good idea remembering she hadn't eaten all day. She walked through to the bedroom, tearing off her clothes as she went into the bathroom. She set the shower as hot as her skin could tolerate. Standing under the spray she allowed the scorching cascade to flow over her body. As she washed the day away, her mind finally started to clear. She stepped out and wrapped a towel around her body and. another around her hair, styling it in a turban.

Walking through to the kitchen, she opened the drawer and took out the take away leaflet she had received the other day. She needed to eat but it was too late to prepare anything. There was a knock on the door, and without thinking, she walked over and opened the door. She was suddenly reminded that she was only wearing a towel, when she looked up at Callum standing there with a bottle of wine.

Callum was taken aback at the sight before him. He didn't think she could look any sexier if she tried. The fact she only had a towel to cover her curves was more than enough for any man to bear, but it was also the innocence she showed on realising how exposed she was. There was a striking, purity about her that almost knocked him off balance.

"I'm sorry," swallowing hard, he reached up, rubbing the back of his neck nervously, "I should have called you first. I just thought as we didn't get to go for that meal." He held out the bottle of Merlot, as a peace offering.

"You had better come in." As nervous as she felt, right now, she was also glad to have some company after the week they had both had. "I'll get dressed." She informed him as she rushed into the bedroom, desperate to cover herself.

"Don't bother on my account." He called after her in a joking tone.

"In your dreams, Sergeant Blake." She called back from the bedroom. "Glasses are in the kitchen above the sink. She shouted.

Five minutes later, she was dressed in grey pyjama shorts, and matching top that slipped of one shoulder. She walked back into the lounge, to see Callum had settled himself on the sofa. He poured out two glasses of wine and she sat on the other end of the sofa distancing herself from him protectively.

He looked up at her as he was pouring the wine and realised once again how beautiful she was. Her long dark curls were still damp and were swept to the side, trailing delicately over one shoulder, leaving the other exposed. He handed her a glass, trying hard to keep his hand steady.

Taking the drink from him, Sienna relaxed back on the sofa. She took a sip and pointed to the take away leaflet on the coffee table. "Have you eaten?"

"Not yet," Callum picked up the leaflet. "but I'm buying." he added.

Sienna raised her glass in a toast fashion. "I'm not arguing."

"Sorry? Hold on, can you repeat that?" He laughed "I never thought I would hear you back out of an argument, are you ill?" he mocked.

Sienna pulled a mock angry face. "No, just hungry, now order the bloody food before I evict you."

Callum managed to fire back at her, "So cute when you're angry." Before she threw a cushion at him.

The food came and, they sat eating Chow Mein and rice, while chatting about anything other than work. They were both glad of the distraction.

Later, pouring the last of the wine, Callum turned to face her. He was sitting closer now than when he had first arrived and Sienna had either not noticed, or not objected.

"Tell me a secret about you." He quizzed.

Sienna laughed, "A secret? Hmm," she thought for a moment, "Okay," she paused again, "I might have just the tiniest phobia of lifts." She gently bit her bottom lip as she spoke, looking guilty at the admission.

Callum laughed out loud. Sienna hit him playfully with the cushion. "Stop it!" she giggled.

"I knew that already." I said, tell me a secret. Something I don't know about you."

There was a brief silence. "Okay, okay let me think." She twisted in her seat bringing her legs up in a foetal position. "I can't cook for toffee." She laughed.

"What? The strong, independent Dr Turner can't even boil an egg?" He beamed, excitedly.

"Correct!" She exclaimed. "In fact, I've even been known to burn water."

"Well I'm an awesome cook, so I'll just have to cook for you one day, won't I?" It was more of a statement than a question.

"We'll see." She tilted her head, with her arm resting on the back of the sofa and considered him for a moment. "Your turn, tell me a secret about you."

He responded to her question, without thinking about it. "I really didn't sleep with as many women as you think but, you were right. It was because I was scared of being close to anyone." Callum was serious when he spoke.

Sienna straightened slightly, "I knew that already too." She responded. Thinking about what he had confessed to, she enquired, "What do you mean 'was' scared?"

He stretched out his arm to meet hers and lightly, but briefly stroked the back of her hand with his finger before pulling away again in case he scared her off, or slapped him.

"Let's just say, I'm getting braver every day." His voice was softer now. He looked into her eyes, unable draw himself away and, if he was honest, he didn't want to.

Sienna's heart was in her throat, she was paralysed to the spot. As hard as she had tried to stop herself, she could feel her self being drawn in by the man sitting opposite her. She had learned over the last week that there was a lot more to him than the man she had berated on the stairs. However, she was too scared to trust him completely or even to trust herself.

Straightening, she broke the spell. "There's hope for you yet." She responded with a gentle tone. "But for now, Sergeant Blake, I need to get some sleep, we have a long day tomorrow."

Callum winked, showing his understanding of the situation, "Quit while I'm ahead eh?"

Sienna dipped her head in agreement, blinking slowly and smiling gently as she did.

They stood up and she walked him to the door. He turned, stepping in close to her so they were almost touching. Their breathing quickened, both nervous, both hopeful. He brought his hand up and swept a curl away, before stroking her face with the back of his hand. He murmured, "Well just, so you know," He drew her closer, "I'm not giving up."

Sienna looked up at him not daring to speak. Her hand was lightly holding his raised arm at the elbow. Callum bent in towards her, placing his hand on the crook of her neck, and kissed her lightly. Sienna responded, parting her mouth allowing him to kiss her more deeply. Callum groaned with pleasure as he pulled away from the kiss, nuzzling her cheek with his nose before repeating "I'm not giving up."

Kissing her cheek tenderly, he wished her goodnight, reminding her to lock her door. Sienna locked the door as promised, placed the empty glass in the sink and turned off the light.

Outside in the carpark, standing under a street light, a solitary figure was leaning against the lamppost, looking up at the apartment block. When he saw the top floor light go out, he turned, and slowly walked away.

Chapter 19

Callum woke early the next morning. Sienna was in his head before he'd even opened his eyes. He rolled over in his bed and lay there thinking about the evening's events. He recalled the way she looked, her smile, her laugh, her playfulness, and that kiss. The full, softness of her lips, the way she kissed, and above all the way she had made him feel. He was as terrified as he was elated. Dr Sienna Turner was amazing, inside, and out and the realisation shook him to the core.

He got up, padded out to the kitchen making himself a coffee and sat on the sofa. Picking up the remote, he switched on the TV and flicked through the channels before turning the TV back off and throwing the remote back on the sofa. He wanted to call Sienna and ask if he wanted to go into work with him again but he was nervous.

What if she regrets me kissing her. She's probably slept on it and decided she doesn't want to know. His fears were taking over again. *She won't even be able to work with me now. Oh, shut up Cal you twat.*

Realising that he was now arguing with himself, he slightly slapped himself on the cheek.

"Get a grip." He told himself out loud, as he headed for the shower. Whilst showering, without realising, Sienna crept back into his thoughts. She was getting under his skin and there was not a damn thing he could do to stop it.

He got dressed, walked out to the kitchen, and put on his watch. He picked up his phone and realised he had a text.

Need to check on something,

see you at the station later.

Doc.

He was both curious and disappointed. He wanted to see her early. Worrying that he'd frightened her off, Callum needed to know she didn't regret that kiss.

At least she sent you a text you prat. He thought, scolding himself. Picking up his keys, he headed out to the station.

----o----

Sienna pulled up outside Elaine Jackson's house to see PC Markowska outside the property. She was younger in years than Sienna and a very good officer according to the DCI. She had arrived at Highbridge a shortly after Sienna. She was offered promotion into CID at her last station but had declined, preferring to stay in uniform where, she felt she could make more difference. There was a shy, quiet air about her, and Sienna liked her immensely.

"Hey Doc, what are you doing here?" PC Markowska was surprised to see her.

"I just need to check on something, is that okay?" Placing her hand on the gate, she stopped before pushing it open. "I won't be long."

"No problem, I'm just here to secure the house now it's finished with. I'll wait until you're done."

"Thanks Cheryl, appreciate it," Sienna turned back to face the officer. "Actually, can you accompany me? I don't want to compromise anything." She added.

Following Sienna, they went into the house and made their way upstairs. The top floor had remained largely untouched, with the murder taking place in the kitchen. It appeared to everyone that nothing had been touched in the rest of the house, so apart from taking prints throughout the property and checking for the usual traces of a disturbance, it was more-or-less left alone.

They went into the main bedroom facing the front of the house which Sienna knew to be where Elaine Jackson slept. She looked around, not entirely sure what she was looking for. Wearing latex forensic gloves, she checked under the bed, the bed clothes, and the wardrobe. PC Markowska's eyes followed her around the room.

Curiosity getting the better of her, she asked, "What exactly are you looking for Doc?"

"I'm not sure," She replied, groaning, as she stretched to reach the shelf at the top of the wardrobe, "but I'll know if I see it."

She went to the chest of drawers and went through each one from the top down. Reaching the drawer second from the bottom, she pulled it out and worked her way through slowly. She felt the smoothness of plastic and pulled the object out. She looked at the plastic sandwich bag and a feeling of dread washed over her. She turned to look at PC Markowska.

"What is it?" The PC responded, anxiously.

Sienna held up the sandwich bag to reveal the contents. The neatly folded knickers were covered in dried blood. "His signature." She muttered solemnly.

She placed the bag on top of the drawers, turned back to PC Markowska again. "I think you'd better get the DCI over here."

Chapter 20

Half an hour later, the new evidence was being taken away and the DCI was standing with Sienna and DI Khatri in the bedroom of Elaine Jackson's house.

"Okay Doc, explain to me what's going on here."

"It's his signature, I've seen it before." She explained, almost excited.

The DCI looked at her directly, waiting for her to continue.

"Something had been niggling at me, it was the depth of the stab wounds. I've seen them before. The pattern is new, but, the depth? That's never changed. The report on the torso of the second body, will show the same wounds."

"You're right, it did," the DCI confirmed sounding confused, "but, you're not making sense, where have you seen it before and what's it got to do with that?" He pointed to the drawer where the sandwich bag had been found.

"Sorry, I'll start from the beginning." She walked over to the edge of the bed, sat down, and continued.

"Just before I moved down here, about six months ago," Sienna recalled, "I was called in to consult on a case in Dorset. Women were being murdered. Three bodies in total were found in the space of two months. There was always something from the previous murder at each scene and always, wrapped neatly in a sandwich bag."

"All the women were blonde and all of them were single and reclusive in nature. As I say, there was no pattern to the wounds, and the bodies were buried in shallow graves as opposed to being put on display. That's why I did not make the connection immediately."

"So, what happened?" The DCI sat next to Sienna on the bed. DI Khatri was taking notes as Sienna spoke.

"The killer was never caught. They simply stopped. I tried to convince the DCI on the case that the killer was stalking his victims online but he wouldn't listen and I was taken off the case."

"Why?" DI Khatri asked.

"Off the record, we clashed from the outset. He was an extreme sexist, who not only didn't like women but was also seemingly opposed to 'head shrinkers spouting their mumbo jumbo' as he put it." Raising one eyebrow she thought for a brief moment, "I had been approached at one point by a female officer who alleged she was being bullied after she rejected his advances. She refused to make it official but I had passed the details unofficially to another senior colleague."

"Nice!" DI Khatri remarked sardonically.

"Quite!" She agreed. Realising she had digressed, she returned to her explanation. "Anyway, as far as I know the case remained open and still is. What I can tell you is, the final victim, was found in a shallow grave in woodlands. She was fully clothed except for her underwear."

The DCI hugged Sienna in excitement. "Well his loss is our gain Doc, this is the best lead we've had so far."

DI Khatri looked on in surprise having never seen this side of the DCI before.

"Right, Baz" The DCI turned to the DI, "I want the top floor and stairs of this house swept again, thoroughly this time. That evidence should have been found earlier." He continued,

"I'll get back to the station and look into the online avenue in more detail." He stopped and turned to Sienna. "We need to find where the second victim was murdered. Find that and we'll find his next 'trophy'."

He went to walk out before turning to Sienna again. "Oh, and Doc?" He was frowning now. "If you go out on your own again while this maniac is on the loose, I'll kick your arse all the way to Timbuctoo."

"Yes, Dad." She chuckled.

"Now come on," He ordered, clapping his hands together, "I'll get Sergeant Blake to get on to Dorset, and see what evidence they can send up. Where is he anyway? Why is he not with you?"

"I left early, I didn't want to impose." She lied.

"Ok, well in future, you stick with him."

Sienna consented and walked out with him to her car.

Chapter 21

Sienna was at her desk going through her own records on her computer from the Dorset case. She had the current file in front of her and was highlighting the similarities and differences between the two cases. Feeling someone watching her, she looked up to see Callum standing in the doorway leaning up against the frame.

"Hi!" She was surprised to see him.

"Hi yourself." He replied, in a not too friendly tone.

Sienna felt nervous. "I take it the DCI has filled you in?"

"He did, but it would have been nice to hear it from you." He replied moodily.

"I thought you'd be busy."

Callum walked into the office and sat down in the chair across the desk from her. "Sienna, don't bullshit me." He spoke gently but the fact he had called her by her real name was not lost on her.

Callum thought for a moment, "If I stepped over the mark last night,"

"You didn't." Sienna interrupted.

"Then what is it?" He leaned forward and leant on the desk. "Why are you avoiding me?"

Confused by his questioning, Sienna frowned. "So, let me get this straight. You kissed me last night and all of a sudden, I'm supposed to run everything I do past you? Exactly how long have you lived in the dark ages?"

Callum, realised how it sounded but was getting too wound up to explain himself properly. "Get over yourself will you. It's not about last night. You went back to the scene of the vicious murder of a single, lone female. You didn't tell anyone where you was going. You proudly stated yourself, the suspect is likely to return to the scene of the crime, so what do you do? You go there alone. Who do you think you are, Miss fucking Marple?"

"I wasn't alone, PC Markowska was there when I arrived. Besides, I am more than capable of looking after myself." She replied indignantly. "If I want protection Sergeant Blake, I'll buy myself a guard dog. It would certainly be better than listening to you, bark orders at me."

"Seriously, Doc? Are you that closed off that you can't even allow anyone to be concerned about you? For a fucking head doctor you need to start practicing what you preach and open the fuck up a little."

Sienna didn't respond, she didn't know what to say.

"Look, like it or not, we have to work together." Callum reasoned. "I like you Si, but if you don't feel the same, I promise it'll be strictly business from now on."

"I never said that, why do you assume to know me so well?" she snapped, in disbelief at his reaction. She was feeling angry and she just wanted the ground to open up beneath her and swallow her whole.

"Know you?" Callum's voice had gone up a level now as he became more frustrated with her. "Oh, trust me, I don't assume to know you at all and why? Because you won't bloody let me that's why." Callum hadn't finished. He got up and paced the floor. Rubbing the back of his head, he turned to Sienna.

"Heaven forbid you could ever let anyone, even knock one brick down from that wall you've built round yourself! In fact, it amazes me how you even had kids!" As soon as he spoke, he knew he'd gone too far.

Sienna, jumped up and flew round the table to the door. Slamming the door shut, she turned to him, glaring angrily. She was hurt and he felt terrible.

"Do you want to know why I have a wall around me? Well I'll bloody well tell you! It's partly because of the father, of those 'kids', who by the way, are the only good thing he ever gave me. I went through hell and back so many times I could get there blind folded by now!" She was shaking, from anger. "I don't want to ever feel that low again, I don't ever want to feel that pain again and most of all, I don't ever want to be the woman on the stairs." She shouted, driving the last point home.

She turned to walk out of the door but Callum beat her to it. Putting his hand on the door to stop her from leaving, he grabbed her, pulling her in close, holding her tightly, kissing and nuzzling the top of her head. He could feel her shaking and he didn't think he had ever felt more ashamed.

"I'm so sorry," he soothed. "I was out of order. I had no right saying what I did, I'm so sorry." Sienna sobbed softly into his chest.

"You're not the only one who's scared of getting close to anyone, Cal." She spoke calmer now. Pulling away from him she added. "I wasn't avoiding you because I had regrets, I was avoiding you in case you did."

Callum smiled and pulled her back in close, nuzzling her cheek, he whispered, "Never, Doc."

"I don't know what this is or where it's going," Sienna continued as he held her close, "but, I want us both to be sure before it goes any further. As you pointed out, we both have to work here, we both have scars and I need to know this is worth the risk."

Callum couldn't argue, as much as he wanted to, he knew she was right. "Okay," He concurred pulling back slightly, holding her face gently in his hands, "you're right, as usual.

We'll take it slowly, but I meant what I said last night, I'm not giving up."

Sienna reached her hand up to his face, urging him to meet hers, "I don't want you too." She whispered as she kissed him passionately.

Chapter 22

Sienna and Callum were in the briefing room listening to the DCI going through the time line again. The dismembered corpse still hadn't been identified, despite a computer-generated picture of the young blonde being released to the media.

The information they received from Dorset and the national database was limited. The station had been badly damaged in a fire and a lot of their records, including computers, had been destroyed. They were also informed the DCI on the case had been dismissed following, sexual harassment and bullying allegations. Sienna was not a bit surprised at this. The Dorset police had promised more information if they had it but it was slow in coming.

Sergeant Fletcher came up from downstairs. "Sir, I think we might have something." He walked across the room and stood with the DCI at the front of the room. Sienna, Callum, and the rest of the team turned to face him.

"There's a Mr and Mrs Wythe at the front desk. They've come down from Manchester. Their daughter," He paused to look at his notebook, refreshing his memory, "Emilie Wythe, is living down here, she's studying law apparently, at the university." He continued.

"They say she usually calls them twice a week but they haven't heard from her. They called in to the shared house she's been staying at and her flatmates assumed she had gone home for the Easter break."

Knowing what was coming Sienna stood up and Callum copied.

"Doc, can you and Cal speak to them?" "Baz, take PC Andrews with you to the house she was staying at, see what you can find out and get her computer." He called after them.

He turned to Sergeant Fletcher, "Thanks for this Dave, can you put them in the soft interview room?"

"Will do Sir." Dave agreed.

Sienna and Callum were about to follow Dave downstairs when the DCI stopped them in their tracks. "Before you go, can I have a word with you both." They looked at each other then back at the DCI. Nodding, they followed him in to his office.

"Take a seat." He offered, in a friendly tone holding out his hand in the direction of the chairs. They sat down, both curious and a little concerned. The DCI walked round to his side of the desk and sat down. Leaning back in his chair, swinging it slightly he finally spoke.

"I don't know if you've heard but the Borough Commander and Chief Super, are trying to expand Highbridge by incorporating a serious crime unit at the station."

"I'd heard a rumour." Callum spoke first. "I thought it was all just pipe dreams though sir."

The DCI nodded and leant forward, "Well as it turns out, the pipe dream might become a reality if he gets his way."

"Will you be heading it Terry?" Sienna questioned.

"So, I've been told." He replied smiling. "The trouble is, it couldn't have come at a worst time."

"This case?" Callum replied.

"Exactly!"

"We need this maniac caught as soon as possible and I know and appreciate you're all working your arses off to make that happen."

"So, I take it there's another problem Terry?" Sienna asked knowingly.

"Two problems, actually and you can help with both."

"I wondered why you was being nice." Sienna joked.

The DCI roared with laughter, "You know me too well. Okay, cards on the table." The DCI clasped his hands in front of him, leaning on the desk as he spoke.

"First Doc, the Super wants you on board as part of the deal. With your qualifications, skill, and reputation, he knows it'll up the game."

"So, I'm good PR?" Sienna responded, sounding a little annoyed.

"Partly, but mainly because you're one of the best there is and he wants the best on his team."

"He's also asked me to recommend good officers to transfer over. Callum I've recommended you. I've been watching the work you've been doing and I'm more than impressed and it hasn't gone unnoticed upstairs either. It'll mean promotion and a salary to match obviously."

Callum looked at Sienna and smiled. She raised her eyebrows and smiled back.

"So, what was the second thing?" Sienna asked, now more than interested.

"Ah, now, the second part *is* PR I'm afraid. The bean shakers are going to be with the Borough Commander, and Chief Super at the Charity Ball tomorrow night." The usually gruff DCI was sheepish as he spoke.

"Oh god!" Sienna interrupted throwing her hand in the air.

"Now, I know you hate these formal gatherings Doc, but please. You'd be doing me and the Super a great favour." The DCI pleaded.

Callum looked at them both confused. "Have I missed something?"

"He wants Cinders and Buttons to go to the ball." She explained, pointing at Callum and then to herself.

Laughing, the DCI continued. "Look, don't think I haven't noticed the chemistry between you two." Still laughing."

"Terry, with all due respect, the only thing you know about chemistry, is the effect of mixing alcohol with tonic water." Sienna exclaimed light heartedly.

DCI Sloane, roared again. "All I need from you two is to put on your best 'bib and tucker', then go and schmooze with the bigwigs. You know the drill."

"Yes, I know the drill and you know I don't schmooze with anyone." Sienna insisted sternly.

"I can vouch for that." Callum added smiling.

Sienna stretched her leg sideways and kicked him in the shin.

The DCI was acutely aware of the spark between them and he smiled approvingly. He had long wanted to see Sienna happy and he had a lot of time and respect for Callum. He hoped a nudge in the right direction might help. So this PR exercise would kill two birds with one nice, neat stone.

"I tell you what, do this for me and I'll make sure no cases come your way for two weeks." He looked thoughtful for a second. "After this case is closed, that is of course. Then, you can have some leave. God knows, Doc, you bloody need a good holiday."

"Okay, Okay!" She held her hands up in surrender. "I'll go to the bloody ball and schmooze until the cows come home if it shuts you up."

The DCI was really laughing now. He looked at Callum. "What about you, you up for this?"

Callum didn't need to be asked twice. "Count me in."

The DCI stood up and walked round the desk and shook Callum's hand. "Thanks Cal, and don't let her bully you too much" he laughed.

As they walked out the door the DCI heard their conversation.

"I suppose you need a whole day off to buy a new dress now." Callum remarked smugly.

"Why, would you like me to pick one up for you too?" Sienna retorted.

"Tell you what, just buy yourself a mini skirt, it'll be a full-length ball gown on you."

"Again with the original height jokes, how old are you exactly? Oh, sorry, I forgot you can't count past ten." Sienna hissed in retaliation.

The DCI laughed again shaking his head. *Looks like I might be buying a new hat after all.* He thought as he went back to the briefing room.

Chapter 23

Down in the soft interview room. Sienna had met with Emilie Wythe's parents. They were considerably authoritarian, speaking only of Emilie's academic achievements. From the information she had extracted from the couple, she deduced that Emilie was sheltered from society and encouraged to study hard. They failed to hide their disappointment that she hadn't made Oxford and had to settle for an 'inferior' university. Sienna guessed Emilie would be only too pleased to go to a university in Outer Mongolia, if it meant getting away from her parents' stifling binds.

The couple had brought a photo of Emilie down with them and had passed it to Callum. He looked at the photo and looked at Sienna and nodded slightly, telling Sienna poor Emilie was indeed the killer's recent victim.

"Did Emilie have any friends in this area Mr and Mrs Wythe?" Sienna questioned, bringing her focus back to the interview.

"No, not at all." Mrs Wythe announced pointedly. "She informed me that she was well acquainted with the people she shared her house with, but she would have been far too busy with her studies to socialise."

"So, she never mentioned a boyfriend?"

"Certainly not!" Mrs Wythe retorted, insulted at the mere suggestion of any fraternisation from her daughter with members of the opposite sex.

Poor girl thought Sienna, imagining what sort of a brief life she had, had.

Emilie's parents did not provide any more information. However, it was enough to know Emilie would have been the ideal target for the killer.

Sienna thanked them for coming in, being so helpful, and assured them, she would send an officer down to speak with them. She knew that once an officer had spoken to them, their dreams of the life they had mapped out for their daughter would be shattered forever. She felt an overwhelming pity for them.

----o----

After the interview Sienna needed to get away for a while. She updated the investigation team on the new information and Emilie's parents had sadly been informed of her death.

She told Callum she was going to look round the shops and he made a joke about seeing her in a week.

Happily walking back from the shopping centre in Highbridge town centre. It had taken her just under an hour to pick out the perfect dress, matching shoes, and a pretty black sequinned clutch bag. *That will shut him up,* she thought smiling, proud of how quick she had made it round the stores.

She stopped to look in a jewellery shop window at a pair of earrings, then turned to head towards her car. She was so wrapped up in her thoughts, she didn't notice the man stepping out from the alley next to the jewellers, watching her and taking photos on his phone as she walked to her car.

Chapter 24

Knocking on the door to the apartment above his the next evening, Callum was surprised, when it wasn't Sienna who answered. She was the image of Sienna however, only younger. "You must be Lilly?" He smiled nervously.

"And you must be Sergeant Callum Blake." Lilly smiled brightly, standing to one side, inviting him in.

"So, you're the man who is trying to tame my mum?" She asked, squinting her eyes in pretend suspicion, before breaking into a broad smile. "I wish you luck" She laughed.

Callum liked her instantly. "Don't suppose you have any tips?" He quipped.

Lilly thought for a moment before answering, "Let her win, and above all," her face was suddenly serious, "for god's sake don't ever let her cook."

Callum threw his head back laughing. "That bad, huh?"

"Put it this way, if she cooked for the prison service, you'd be out of a job."

Still laughing, Callum could see where she got her sense of humour from.

"I heard that madam, you're never too old to be grounded you know."

Callum turned, to face the voice behind him, and nearly fell over.

"Wow!" He stuttered. "Si, you look amazing." His heart had doubled in pace, and he was completely mesmerised by her.

"Will I do?" She murmured, nervously.

Sienna was dressed in a long deep red fitted satin dress which hugged her curves. The bottom tapered out in a mermaid style. The low neckline was shaped, tastefully accentuating her breasts. Sienna turned and the back of the dress plunged to just below her waist, just inches above her perfectly shaped bottom. A delicate white gold chain which held the dress across the shoulders, fell loosely down the centre of her back. Her hair was styled elegantly in a low bun with loose ringlets cascading down at the sides framing her face perfectly. She twirled back and Callum walked over to her and held her close, nuzzling her cheek before kissing her lightly on the lips. "I don't think I've ever seen anything more beautiful" he remarked honestly.

"And, on that note I think it's time for me to go." Interrupted Lilly behind them breaking the spell.

Feeling protective of Sienna's daughter, Callum insisted on walking her down to her car, especially knowing what might lie out there. In the lift, Lilly, turned to face him, asking seriously this time. "You really like mum, don't you?"

Callum took a deep breath in, "I do," pausing thoughtfully, "more than I ever thought possible." He was speaking the truth. Sienna had come to mean a great deal to him in such a short space of time, but he was struggling to process it, it had hit him so fast.

As if reading his mind, Lilly replied, "She's just as scared as you, if not more so." Callum looked down at Lilly, not surprised that she had guessed he was afraid. She was her mother's daughter after all.

Lilly continued, "All I can say is, mum seems happy, so I'm happy. Just don't rush her, or yourself." Callum smiled in agreement, understanding this was her approving of him. "and don't try too hard to protect her." She added.

"I learned that much already." He replied, with a regretful tone.

"She's fought her own battles and won for far too long to start letting somebody do it for her. There's no point fighting her on it because, trust me, you'll never win. Also, be honest with her. Mum respects honesty above anything else." Lilly's advice was heartfelt and it was appreciated.

Making sure Lilly was safely in her car, Callum came back into the apartment. Sienna was standing at the kitchen counter with her back to him. He was in a trance. She was perfect from head to toe. He walked over to her and put his arm round her waist from behind. Nuzzling into her neck. "Ready? "

She turned while in his arms "Ready." she smiled.

The rest of the evening was like a whirlwind. Arriving at the venue, Callum felt more than proud to have this beautiful woman on his arm. He looked striking in his dinner suit, and got more than a few looks from other women. His deep blue eyes sparkled and his smile stood out, making Sienna's heart flutter every time she looked at him.

Sienna met with the DCI, Chief Superintendent, the Borough Commander, and other VIP's. Callum went to refresh her drink, giving her space to entertain their ideas and many questions they had regarding the new plans. He stood with Dave Fletcher as he watched her. He was hypnotised by her beautiful smile, as she listened intently to their ramblings, nodding in all the right places, playing the perfect host. Sienna briefly looked over at him, he winked at her smiling broadly, she returned the smile before diverting her attention back to her audience.

"You've got it bad mate." Dave, broke through Callum's thoughts. They had been friends for nearly ten years, rising through the ranks together. They had been through a lot and trusted each other implicitly.

"You think, Dave?" Callum replied, not really sure how to answer.

"Mate, I've known you for a decade and I have never seen you look at, or talk about anyone like you do the Doc." Dave was shaking his head, smirking, knowing full well he was right.

"Just admit it, she's got to you, hasn't she?" He looked over to where Sienna was standing and continued. "Look, I don't blame you, look at her. What's not to like. You're lucky I'm happily married or you wouldn't have stood a chance." Dave joked.

Callum laughed with him then said seriously, "Dave, it's not like that, I mean, it is but, it's not just that." He was rambling, trying to explain to his best friend how he felt but, not knowing how to begin.

Dave stepped in to save him, "I know it's not like that. She's more than a pretty face and that's exactly why she's got to you." Dave stopped to consider Callum's predicament.

"Look mate, you gotta take a gamble at some point. You ain't getting any younger. Just roll with it." Encouraging him further, Dave added, "The Doc is nothing like the others Cal, she's class. If you don't take the plunge, you'll regret it trust me."

Dave looked round and caught the eye of his wife looking on nervously, standing with a rather drunk officer. "Look I need to rescue the missus before she commits murder," holding out his hand to shake Callum's, "but take my advice, don't let her slip through your fingers." He patted Callum on the back and walked off to save his wife from the drunken advances of the inebriated officer.

Callum got Sienna a fresh drink and walked over to the group she was with. "Excuse me gentleman, do you mind if I borrow Dr Turner for a moment?" The group nodded and Callum led Sienna off. "I think that's enough schmoozing to satisfy the bigwigs. Come and dance with me."

Sienna allowed Callum to lead her to the dance floor which was filled with officers of varying ranks, and gender, all dancing drunkenly either with their partners or each other.

'When I'm gone' was being played out across the dance floor, and Callum took Sienna in his arms as they danced slowly, talking together, laughing, and holding each other close.

Sienna was feeling light headed from too much champagne, and she held on to Callum tighter for support. He placed his fingers under her chin, gently lifting her face to look at him, bending close, her nuzzled into her face and kissed her slowly as they swayed to the haunting music. They were so wrapped up in the moment that they forgot they were in a room full of colleagues.

The DCI had watched the event unfold before him, *Well it's about bloody time.* He thought, happily accepting his own praise for his part in getting them together. He was also equally pleased with himself, for persuading Sienna to speak with the powers that be, about the stations future plans.

The VIPs were all more than impressed with Dr Turner earlier and she had worked wonders on them. Plans had already been arranged to meet, discuss plans further and 'dot the I's and cross the t's'. It couldn't have gone any better.

Dave, danced with his wife, holding her to him like she was made of gold. They swept past the couple, and Dave winked his approval at Callum, making him suddenly remember where they were. "I think we've been sussed." He remarked, looking down at Sienna.

She looked around and noticed that a few of their colleagues were watching them. "Oops!" she giggled, a little drunkenly.

"Champagne gone to your head Si?" He asked her, amused.

Sienna murmured as she leant her head, on Callum's chest. He savoured every moment. The feel of her body against him, the light scent of her perfume and the softness of her skin as he lightly stroked her back as they danced. It was a perfect evening all round.

They arrived back at Sienna's apartment just after midnight. Sienna was tired, still a little drunk, but she was happy. She opened the door and they went in to the apartment without speaking. Closing the door, she turned to face Callum. He walked towards her slowly as she walked backwards until she reached the wall. He placed one hand on the crook of her neck and the other on the wall behind her.

"You were amazing tonight Si." He exclaimed. He took in her body and then her face with his eyes. "God you're so beautiful." He was breathless and his eyes were dilated, drawing Sienna in. She was lost.

He kissed her slowly at first and then passionately. She responded allowing him to search her mouth with his tongue. She felt helpless to stop him and, in that moment, she didn't care. Kissing her neck, he ran his hand down her side, tracing the shape of her curves. Sienna lifted her head back and groaned as he kissed her throat up to her chin and then, her mouth. He stopped, completely breathless, fighting hard to stop himself from going any further.

"Every part of me wants to stay Si, but I can't. Oh god, I want to but I can't."

Sienna opened her eyes and looked at him, waiting for him to explain.

"We've both had a lot to drink this evening," As he spoke, he rested his forehead on hers, gently running his finger over her breasts, down the front of her body to her stomach. "I don't want it to be a drunken night. You mean more to me than that."

Sienna smiled softly. She understood, and felt relieved. She felt the same, and appreciated the respect he had for her. She reached up and kissed him again.

"Thank you." She replied gently.

They kissed again and Callum left, promising to see her the next morning.

Chapter 25

Waking to a loud knocking at her door, Sienna got up, threw on her robe and shuffled sleepily to the door. Her head was a little sore from last night's champagne and she winced as the light from the front room window hit her eyes. She opened the door to the postman.

"Sorry to wake you. I couldn't get this last one through the letter box." The postman held out a small padded envelope.

She thanked him, taking the packet, and closed the door. She picked up the rest of the mail off of the mat and placed it on the counter. She put on some coffee and as it brewed she went to the bathroom, washed, and brushed her teeth. She reached into the medicine cabinet above the sink and took out two tablets. Filling the glass with water, she swallowed the tablets and went back to the kitchen.

Pouring a coffee, she sat at the breakfast bar and assessed the package before her. She was curious as she wasn't expecting anything. Carefully opening the package and pulling out what was inside, she jumped, nearly dropping the contents. Slowly, she placed it on the counter, picked up her mobile and dialled.

"Cal?" There was a tremor in her voice. "Can you come up? I've had a delivery." She looked down at the package, a wave of nausea enveloped her.

"It's from the killer." She finished, trying her hardest to sound calm.

Callum was at her door in seconds. He was wearing only unbuttoned jeans and his hair was ruffled from sleep. He looked panicked, but alert. As soon as Sienna answered, he took her in his arms and held her close.

"What's happened? Are you ok? What do you mean from the killer?" He was reeling off questions one after the other without giving her the chance to answer. His eyes looked startled. He was afraid for her. Sienna needed to calm him down so she could speak to him properly and get him to focus. She placed her finger on his lips and hushed him soothingly.

"It's ok, I'm fine, it was delivered by the postman." She reassured him.

Leading him over to the sofa, she urged him to sit down. She went to the breakfast bar and returned with the package and forensic gloves. She handed him the gloves so his prints would not contaminate any evidence. There was a silver mobile phone, covered in dried blood. The battery had been taken out of the phone and placed with the phone, neatly wrapped inside a sandwich bag.

"I think it's Elaine Jackson's" She gulped dryly.

Callum was astounded and impressed at her calmness. She went back, got him a coffee, and placed it on the coffee table before him. She then explained the delivery to him, before phoning through to the DCI to explain what had happened.

The DCI told her he would be right there and asked if she was safe. She reassured him that she had called Callum who was there with her now.

When she finished, she went back to Callum who pulled her down on to his lap and held her protectively. She leaned into his bare muscular chest for a moment before jumping up. This time, she sounded panicked.

"Oh god, Lilly!" She started. "If he knows where I live, he might have been watching last night and followed her." She rushed back to her phone and dialled.

Callum was up standing next to her now. Thankfully, Lilly answered the phone after four rings. She assured her mum that she was fine and promised she would go to Jack's until her mum contacted her again. Relieved, she put the phone down and Callum hugged her.

Feeling calmer, she remembered that Callum was barely dressed. Giggling, she remarked, "I think it might be a good idea if you go and put some clothes on."

Callum looked down at himself and realised he wasn't even wearing shoes. "Okay." He smiled. "I'll be five minutes. You lock the door behind me, and use the bloody spy hole before you answer." He ordered, recalling the night she had opened the door to him in her towel.

Sienna promised that she would and Callum sped off to get dressed.

Chapter 26

The DCI had arrived with DI Khatri and PC Markowska. The PC hugged Sienna and Sienna thanked her, assuring her she was fine before recalling the morning to the rest of the room.

The DCI looked at the wrapped phone and battery. "Why take the battery out?" He wondered out loud.

Wearing gloves, he took out the phone and replaced the battery, pressing the power button the phone burst into life. The DCI turned the screen of the phone to face Sienna and repeated his question.

"Can I see?" Sienna requested, putting on gloves as she spoke. The DCI handed her the phone and she began scrolling through the phone as she spoke.

"He wants me to see something." She explained.

She found what she was looking for on the phone and she went quiet. Her hand was visibly shaking as she pressed play on the video.

Loud petrifying screams emitted from the phone and Sienna brought her hand up to cover her mouth. She gripped the phone tightly in both revulsion and anger.

Callum, who was sitting next to her looked over her shoulder and saw the horror that was unfolding before him. Gently, he went to take the phone from Sienna but she was frozen. With her grip not releasing, he spoke reassuringly. "Si, give me the phone, it's okay." A tear spilled from her eye and ran down her cheek. She let go of the phone allowing Callum to take it who, in turn handed it to the DCI.

The DCI viewed the rest of the video. Even as hardened as he was, he could not help but reel in horror at the images on the screen. Emilie Wythe, was tied to what looked like a kitchen table, she was naked, and was being tortured. Brutally and horrifically tortured. All the while it was being filmed for prosperity on Elaine Jackson's phone. The DCI and the others viewed the rest of the footage which was eleven disturbing minutes long in stunned silence. While you could see she was being tortured, you could not see the perpetrator of the violence, who was holding the phone as he carried out the vile act.

After a while, PC Markowska was the first to speak. "Why has he sent the phone to Dr Turner?" Her voice was dry and cracked as she spoke.

Sienna got up and got the PC a drink. She accepted it gratefully and drank. "He's angry with me, maybe he saw me in the press conference we delivered."

The DCI carried on the conversation from Sienna, "Plus, he always leaves a trophy from the previous victim with the next one. Looks like he may be planning ahead this time." The concern in his voice, was evident to everyone in the room.

"But why?" Callum asked, his heart was thumping, fighting to burst through his chest.

DI Khatri also questioned the DCI's prediction. "Doc doesn't even fit his type. She's not blonde, she's certainly not timid. No offence, Doc."

"None taken, Baz. However, I'm a woman, consulting on his horrific murders and I don't show fear. Therefore, I'm not giving him what he wants." She pointed out before adding, "It's an insult to him and he is reacting in the only way he knows."

She turned to Callum and continued. "It's like you said before Cal, I'm closed off. He can't stand it that I don't react emotionally."

"Si, I didn't mean,"

"No, it's fine. You were right." She reassured him, "I know it's how I protect myself. The only emotion I show is anger. My best defence is to either fight or shut down. But these girls are terrified. That's the reaction he wants from me, even if it does mean changing his type."

"Well that's it, I can't have you put at risk, I'm going to have to take you off the case." The DCI explained, angry but full of concern.

True to form, Sienna was suddenly fuming. Jumping up, she struggled to keep her composure. "What the hell is that going to solve? The damage has been done now. Taking me off the case is giving him exactly what he wants!" She was pacing the floor angrily.

"Besides, if I am on the case, I am surrounded by officers practically twenty-four hours a day. If you want me safe, then I am better off staying involved."

She marched over to the kitchen and got herself a glass of water. She knew she needed to keep it together, but right now she could commit murders herself.

The room was quiet until Callum spoke. "If it helps, I can stay here on the sofa." he offered, looking between Sienna and the DCI. "Doc's right, she's safer surrounded by us than she is sitting it out here on her own." He added convincingly.

Thinking for a while, the DCI finally gave in. "Okay, but you go nowhere without reporting in. No one woman crusades. You stay with Callum the whole time. If he's not available, you stay at the station." Knowing Sienna's stubborn, and sometimes maverick nature, he reiterated the point. "I mean it, Doc. One whiff of you going off grid and I'll pull you off this case so fast, you won't have time to blink."

Relieved, Sienna calmed down. "I promise."

Chapter 27

DI Khatri and PC Andrews had visited the shared house where Emilie Wythe had been staying, the previous day. They had retrieved her laptop and it was being fast tracked for examination by the forensic IT team.

CCTV had been collated from Sienna's apartment block and was being viewed. It was a slow process as they had to go back as far as the press conference four days previous. Sienna had given her official statement regarding the delivery that morning. The video from the phone had been downloaded for analysis and the phone was sent to forensics.

Sienna was in her office watching the video over and over, trying to pick up on anything, anything that would throw more light on the killer's character. The images on the screen disturbed her more every time she watched them. She tried hard not to think about the anguish and pain Emilie had gone through before he had finally released her from her horrendous suffering, by killing her.

Callum walked in carrying a paper carrier bag. Sienna looked up wearily. She both looked, and felt like she'd been hit by a train, but she knew she had to keep going.

Looking at Sienna, his heart went out to her. He would give anything to take all this away from her. He wanted to sweep her up in his arms and carry her off somewhere far away from all this. At the same time, he knew that trying to shield her was the last thing she would want. All he could do was be there for her.

"Right you," he held up the bag smiling, trying to put some light back in the room. "If I can't stop you, at least have a break."

"I can't, I know there is something on this footage, something I'm missing."

"Well, you're not going to get anywhere on an empty stomach." He was being firm with her, he needed to pull her away for just a while. He knew she needed at least that, even if she couldn't see it.

"Please Si, just ten minutes. Try and eat something and then I'll sit with you. You never know an extra pair of eyes might help."

Knowing he wasn't about to give up on her, Sienna decided it would be quicker to let him have his way for ten minutes rather than spending a whole day arguing over it.

"Okay, ten minutes, but I really don't think I could eat anything."

"Just try woman."

"Okay, okay!" She relented, frustrated but pleased for the distraction he provided.

Callum set the bag down and walked round to Sienna, bending over, placing his hands on each arm of the chair, he wheeled her round to the front of the desk away from the screen.

Sienna chuckled "You're a crazy fool, you know that?"

"Thanks for the diagnosis, Doc." He beamed, pleased he had managed to get her to smile, at least for a little while.

Pulling out two coffees from the bag, he produced two freshly made sandwiches. He handed her a wrapped sandwich filled with peppered chicken, mayonnaise, and watercress. Sienna was surprised. "How did you know?" She asked looking up at him.

"I spoke to Lilly, she told me it was your favourite." He grinned.

"Ah, I have a spy in the nest." She laughed.

"Seriously, we're worried about you, Si."

"I know, but I'm fine honestly. I just need to focus my attention on this case." She pointed towards her monitor. "Before anyone else has to suffer." She finished.

Callum picked up her hand and held it to his lips, kissing it lightly as he closed his eyes. Opening them again, he spoke. "Si, I get it, but we're all in this together. This is not just your battle." He stroked her face softly. Let me help you. Don't shut us out. Don't shut me out."

Sienna leant forward and rested her forehead on his and closed her eyes. She knew he was right, but it was so hard. This was personal to her now. This maniac had violated her personal space, made both her, and her family feel threatened. She was not about to let that go. "I'll try." She promised.

Finishing her coffee, she only managed half of the sandwich but she was grateful all the same. Callum was right, not that she'd admit it. She did feel a little better. "Ten minutes are up." She announced, looking at her watch.

"So punctual!" Callum mocked, as he leant forward, kissing her slowly as he stroked the nape of her neck.

Breaking away, he jumped up, wheeling her back round to the screen in the same way. "Come on then little miss stubborn, back to it." He then grabbed the other chair, and wheeled it round next to her and sat down. Sienna moved the mouse and clicked play on the footage.

They sat watching for the next five minutes, when Callum straightened. "Go back a bit Doc," he requested, leaning closer towards the screen, ready to focus closely on what he had just spotted.

Sienna went back as directed. "There!" He pointed at the screen.

Looking at Calum and then the screen, Sienna wasn't sure what he was pointing at.

"Look at her face." He pointed again. Sienna squinted, looking closer, and she finally saw what Callum had seen. She sat back suddenly, gasping as she put her hand over her mouth. She looked at Callum put her hands on either side of his face, and kissed him firmly.

"See! An extra pair of eyes, and actually listening to an expert, and look what happens." He joked.

Sienna slapped him playfully. They viewed the footage one more time, before they both rushed up to the incident room.

Upstairs they had everyone's attention. The footage was being played on a large screen in the room, with Callum holding the remote as he scrolled through to the part he had pointed out downstairs. He paused the image. Callum and Sienna could see it as clear as day now on the larger screen, but the rest of the room were still bewildered. Callum walked over to the screen, and pointed Emilie's face. "She's pleading for her life." He explained.

Still confused, DI Khatri frowned, "Well she would be."

Callum looked at Sienna and Sienna spoke next. "She's not pleading to the killer, she's looking past him, away from the direction of the phone."

The penny had dropped. "There's two of them!" the DCI jumped, almost shouting at the realisation.

"Exactly!" Callum exclaimed.

Sienna interjected. "She doesn't look at him once, throughout the whole footage. She only ever looks to the other person in the room." She stood up and walked over to where Callum was standing and turned to face the room. "Every time, she looks past the camera."

She looked round the room and explained further. Pointing to PC Mitchell, a young female officer, who was going through files but listening to Sienna.

"Claire, if you're being followed, out on the street, or even if you were just lost, which gender would you be more likely to go to for help?" She asked the officer.

"A woman, every time." PC Mitchell responded without having to think about her answer.

"Exactly," She looked at Callum who winked at her. She smiled gratefully to him and turned to the rest of the room.

"The partner's a woman?" DI Khatri enquired.

"The partner is a woman." Sienna repeated, answering the DI. "She will probably be submissive to him. She's going along with it because she's either been conditioned, or she simply has no choice." Sienna continued. "This woman, will be totally dependent on him, doing his fetching and carrying. He may even have her injected into the investigation somehow. An onlooker for example."

The DCI joined Callum and Sienna, "That's excellent, well done you two." Turning to the team he clapped his hands together excitedly and began instructing them on how to proceed.

"I want every piece of footage we have viewed again. I want two of you to go back to the victim's friends, families, employers, everyone. Find out if they had any new female friends. How are we doing with Emilie Wythe's laptop?"

"It's ready Sir, I chased it up myself. I was just on my way down there now." PC Andrews gloated.

"Okay, well get a move on." Clapping his hands together again, "Come on you lot let's get to work."

The incident room came alive as everyone went about their duties. Now they had a new direction, there was a refreshing air of confidence in the room. Morale had just been lifted ten-fold.

The DCI turned to Callum and Sienna. "Well done you two," He winked at them and smiled as he turned walking back to his office, "Good teamwork." He called back.

Chapter 28

The pair arrived back at Callum's apartment just after eight that evening. They were both exhausted. Callum went for a shower while Sienna waited in the lounge. A little while later, he came back into the room, wearing grey jogging bottoms. He sat on the sofa and pulled Sienna over to him so she was sitting across his lap. He kissed her deeply as he run his hand up the outside of her thigh to her waist. Nuzzling into her cheek, he whispered. "What, are you doing to me Dr Turner?"

She tilted her head back so she could look at him. "Is it going to be difficult for you sleeping on my sofa? I'll be quite safe on my own if it's awkward for you."

Callum stroked her face and let his hand rest on her neck. "The only difficulty I'll have, is staying on that sofa." He smiled, before adding, "But, I'll do whatever it takes."

Happy with his answer, Sienna nodded.

"Tell you what, why don't I cook for us here, and then we can go up to yours?" He offered.

"What? You mean, you don't want me to cook for you?" She questioned in fake surprise.

Pretending to look horrified, Callum chimed, "If you didn't like me, you only had to say!"

She playfully slapped his chest.

"I can't help it if your reputation includes poisoning people, Doc." He protested.

"Shut up and cook." She ordered.

They ate a wild mushroom risotto, and Sienna was loathed to admit, he really was a good cook.

After they laid together on the sofa, kissing and caressing each other tenderly. They talked for hours, swapping tales of each other's pasts. Callum recalled his army days, when he got the eagle tattoo on his back, which Sienna admitted she really liked. "It's very... you." She told him as she sat across him, tracing the outline of the eagle with her finger, while he lay on his front, savouring every moment of her touch.

He told her about the pranks he used to pull and had pulled on him, about friends that he had lost in Afghanistan. He talked about his son Dominic, how he missed him every day, but loved the time he had video calling him and speaking to him on the telephone. He looked forward to his visits in the summer holidays when he would usually stay for a month.

Sienna told stories of her school days and the trouble she used to get into. Callum was quite surprised to hear what a rebel of a child she was. She spoke about her love of animals, the riding accidents she'd had, the places she had been too. She too, spoke about her children and how proud she was of them. She even managed to open up a little, talking about her years in care.

They didn't make it to Sienna's apartment, but instead fell asleep on the sofa in each other's arms.

Callum woke later and looked down at the stunning woman in his arms, laying there for over an hour, watching her sleep peacefully. He listened to her breathe and murmur occasionally as she dreamt. He desperately wanted to wake her and make love to her. Instead he got up and carried her to his bedroom. Laying her gently on the bed, covering her with the duvet. Kissing her tenderly on the forehead, Callum went back to the lounge and laid on the sofa. He covered himself with a throw and slept on the sofa for the next few hours. The last thing he thought about before he went to sleep, was Sienna and the evening they had just spent together. He couldn't remember ever feeling so close to anyone in his entire life.

Sienna opened her eyes and laid still for a moment. She was confused with the fog of sleep, still clouding her thoughts. She lifted her head wearily, trying to focus her eyes on her surroundings. She didn't recognise where she was. As her head cleared, she remembered she was at Callum's last night.

"Morning sleepy head."

She looked up to see Callum, leaning up against the bedroom door holding two steaming mugs of coffee. He walked over to her, placing the mugs down on the bedside table, he sat down gently on the bed next to her. Seeing her confusion. He laughed.

"Don't worry, I didn't have my wicked way with you while you slept." He pointed at the bed, "I woke up and carried you in here. I slept on the sofa, and in case you're wondering, I didn't peek once." He eyed the shape of her body under the covers as he spoke.

She, lifted the duvet slightly to see she was still dressed before replying, "Well thank you for your remarkable restraint." pulling herself up to a sitting position. "You didn't need to carry me in here though. I would have been quite happy out there." She indicated towards the lounge.

He picked up a mug of coffee and handed it to her. "What and have you think I'm not a gentleman?" He questioned with a teasing smile. "I'd never hear the end of it."

Sienna sipped the hot liquid, grateful for the instant hit of caffeine. "Mm," she agreed, raising an eyebrow, giving him a sideways glance" and I would have made sure everyone knew about it too." She threatened, smiling.

He leant across her and kissed her forehead. "I wouldn't put it past you."

He straightened "Right, come on lazybones, let's see if I can beat your best time." Sienna looked confused.

"Well I know you won't want to miss your run, you didn't get out there yesterday and," his eyes narrowed as he lowered his head towards her eyeing her suspiciously, "I'm not letting you go alone."

She broke into a smile. "Do you even run? I've never seen you accomplish anything more than a fast walk. "

"Hey!" He argued "I'm ex-army remember. I was running 15 miles while you were sitting in a stuffy university with your cute little nose in a book."

"Yes, but you're a police sergeant now and everyone knows the only running they do is back to their office to get out of the hard work!"

Sienna was on form and Callum was over the moon to see her back to her quick-witted, obstinate self. He took her mug from her pushed her back on the bed. Pinning her down under the duvet, he knelt over her holding her arms back.

"You're a cheeky mare." they were both laughing and Sienna was squirming to get free. "You'll pay for that."

"Promises, promises 'Sergeant Sedentary'." She squealed as he tickled her through the duvet.

"You're a piece of work you know that." Callum lowered himself so he was laying on top of her. He propped himself up on his elbows. "One of these days..."

He left the sentence open, lowering himself more he kissed her so passionately, he didn't want to stop. Pulling back, he nuzzled her neck. *One of these days,* he thought hopefully.

Half an hour later they were racing along the sand track surrounding the golf course. Callum was faster than her but Sienna beat him for stamina, easily out running him. Of course, she teased him for it all the way back.

Chapter 29

Arriving in CID, the DCI's office door was closed and the blinds were pulled down. Not giving much thought, Sienna sat with PC Andrews going through the new reports and statements.

PC Dale Andrews was an awkward looking young man in his early twenties who, claimed to know a lot more than he actually did. Thinking himself worthy of bigger and better things, being a cut above his colleagues, he often challenged other's ideas, and even the commands of his superiors. Sienna had already seen an example of this in the initial briefing. Callum had torn strips off him on several occasions for not being a team player.

He had once put a fellow officer in danger by going off on his own, thinking tackling graffiti crime was beneath him. He had left his colleague alone in an unsavoury part of the Brickfield estate. The stranded officer became surrounded by youths who proceeded to knock the lone officer to the floor, before delivering a beating which resulted in two broken ribs and being covered in spray paint.

Sienna was trying to explain why she had profiled the new unknown suspect as a female. However, PC Andrews apparently knew better.

"So, what, we're supposed to focus all our time and attention, looking for a woman 'cos you read some books on psychos and have a hunch about a victim being more likely to plead with a female?" PC Andrews sneered.

Not appreciating his tone or impertinence, Sienna insisted firmly, "Criminal Psychology is not about hunches, PC Andrews. Extensive studies going back centuries have gone into studying behaviour. Also, for the record, I have done far more than read a 'few books'."

PC Andrews looked at Sienna as if she was something he had stepped in. "Well, I think we should be working on hard evidence and not wasting time listening to some bird who watches too many American cop shows. Just cos you've got the DCI drooling over you, believing your shit, don't mean the rest of us have to." He was being deliberately insulting.

Sienna was incensed "If you think a PhD, two master's degrees, extensive training in police procedures, not to mention, twenty years of experience working with police forces across the country is on the same level as watching 'Law and Order' then you need to go back to Police college and do your homework." She hadn't finished.

"Take my advice. Before you give an opinion on anything, especially to a colleague, I suggest you learn the facts first. Sometimes, and particularly in your case PC Andrews, it's better that you say nothing and just *look* stupid, rather than speaking and removing any doubt." Sienna stood up. "Oh, and when you do finally manage to pull your head out if your backside, you may want to buy yourself a dictionary and look up the word 'respect'."

"You stuck up bitch." PC Andrews hissed.

Sienna laughed, "You'll have to do better than that to upset me, PC Andrews, but you don't have the knowledge or the vocabulary." She turned to walk away to see Callum standing there. He had heard everything.

Fuming, he stormed over, his fists were clenched and he headed straight for the young PC. "My office. Now!" he bellowed.

PC Andrews was too stupid to realise when to be quiet and thought he could push his luck further. "Oh, so we all have to jump to her attention 'cos you're giving her one?"

Callum lunged forward, but Sienna jumped in between them. "No Cal!" She pleaded calmly but firmly.

He stopped and looked at her. His breathing was fast and he was bent forward at the shoulders. He looked eerily menacing. Sienna looked in his eyes, calming him with her soft smile.

"By the book." She whispered. He blinked slowly, calming himself down, and nodded.

Side stepping around her, he pointed in PC Andrew's face. "Another word from you and you'll be out of a job so fast, you won't know what's hit you. Now get in my office before I really lose it." He boomed.

The penny had finally dropped and PC Andrews had realised he had gone way too far. He put his head down and walked past the pair. "Sir!" Obstinately, heading towards the door.

Callum walked over to Sienna and placed his hand on the crook of her neck, leaning forward with his forehead on hers. "I'm sorry."

"It's okay, Cal, but I can hold my own,"

"I know, I heard." He smiled, "But he needs taking down a few pegs." He was calmer now.

"You're right, he does, but do it the right way."

The DCI had heard the commotion and come out of his office. "'Bout time he got ripped a new one. You need to speak to him." He bellowed before continuing, "But before you do, we have a problem. Can you come in?"

They walked into the office and DI Khatri was sitting in the corner. He had a serious expression and greeted them soberly as they walked in.

"Take a seat." The DCI directed as he sat back in his chair.

They sat down, both equally concerned now. "What is it, Terry?" Sienna questioned.

"What I'm about tell you, does not leave this room." He looked between the other three, waiting for their acknowledgement before he continued.

"The IT forensics team have come back with information on Emilie Wythe's laptop. She'd been in the same chat room as Elaine Jackson."

DI Khatri interrupted, "When PC Andrews and I collected the laptop from Emilie's house all of the information on the laptop was intact. The chat room account was password protected, so we couldn't gain access to it at the time. We were hoping forensics could get into it. However," He leaned in towards them. "The chat room link and history had been deleted, in between arriving in the incident room and being taken down to forensics." PC Andrews had signed the off the evidence and taken it down there himself.

"Oh, my god!" Sienna exclaimed.

"He's our suspect?" Callum, was completely taken back by this new information.

The DCI shrugged and continued. "Forensics were still able to gain access some of the information and they have found the IP address of the last person she spoke to. Their tracing it now, we should get confirmation any time soon."

DI Khatri interjected again, "For obvious reasons we want to keep this quiet. In the meantime, we need to speak to PC Andrews."

Sienna was still not convinced. "He doesn't fit the profile. Okay, so his attitude leaves a lot to be desired, but he's not clever enough to carry out crimes of this magnitude."

The DCI agreed with her. "You're right but there's a reason he wiped that drive and we need to find out what that is." He stood up and walked round the desk and perched on the end.

"Doc, are you certain the partner is a woman?"

"As sure as I can be Terry." Thinking carefully, she went on. "As far as PC Andrew's is concerned however, he thinks he's far too important to be anyone's submissive. He proved that just now. However, he doesn't have the intelligence to be the dominant member either."

"Docs right." Callum cut in. "Even when I collared him he still challenged me. That shows both stupidity and disrespect."

The DCI agreed and turned to DI Khatri, "Baz, I want you and Cal to speak to him, keep it on the QT." He reiterated.

"Doc, I want you with me while they're with him. You're already under threat and if he does have something to do with this, you're in danger here too." The DCI was adamant.

----o----

PC Andrews was downstairs waiting nervously to be reprimanded over his comments earlier. He was pacing the floor nervously wondering how he could talk his way out of this one. He was telling himself that he would be okay as he was far too valuable to the team, to be taken off the investigation when Callum and DI Khatri entered the office.

"Sit down!" Callum ordered sternly.

PC Andrews started to protest. "Sir, I'm sorry, I was out of line, it won't..."

"That can wait. Sit!"

PC Andrews sat and was looking nervous. DI Khatri and Callum sat opposite him. DI Khatri regarded him closely and begun.

"When we collected Emilie Wythe's laptop from her house, you were with me when I checked it correct?"

Looking confused, he stammered, "Y-Yeah, that's right."

"What do you remember seeing on the laptop?"

"I don't get you."

DI Khatri rolled his eyes, *the Doc's right about this one.* He thought. "What-information-was-on-the-laptop?" He questioned, rounding his words as if PC Andrews was hard of hearing.

PC Andrews was perplexed *Who the fuck does he think he is?* "Usual stuff, files, and websites, along with a chatroom account. What is this?" He demanded.

"Watch you're tone PC Andrews." Callum barked.

DI Khatri continued. "We brought the laptop here and took it up to the incident room. Is that correct?"

"Yes, yes that's correct, wh..."

"You signed off the evidence bag and took the laptop down to forensics, yes?"

PC Andrews nodded.

"You took it straight there, you didn't deviate, put it down anywhere, give it to anyone else?"

Suddenly, PC Andrews eyes widened, he started to rub his temple. "I-I, took it straight to forensics."

"You're sure?"

"Yes!"

"So, can you explain why, when forensics looked at the laptop, the chat room account and history had been deleted?"

PC Andrews immediately sat up straight. He looked from DI Khatri and Callum in a state of confusion and panic. He didn't answer, he couldn't.

----o----

"So, Doc," The DCI started quizzically, "how are things with Callum sleeping on your sofa?"

Subtle, Sienna thought smiling. "Well, he's still sleeping on the sofa, if that's what you're wondering Terry." She retorted.

The DCI Laughed out loud, "I just want you kids to get along that's all."

"Kids? Terry, we're both nearing forty." She was laughing now, but feeling a little embarrassed. "But yes, we're getting on very well thank you, and before you ask, he's being a perfect gentleman."

"Well he'd be too scared not too. Takes a brave man to take on Dr Turner and live to tell the tale." He was laughing as he spoke. "Seriously though, make sure he treats you right. Any problems, you come to me."

Sienna was touched. "Thanks Terry, but I can…"

"Look after yourself. I know." he interrupted. "Even so, you know where I am. Although, you do know he's besotted with you, don't you? I've never seen him like this with anyone."

Embarrassed, Sienna dipped her eyes unable to look at the DCI, "Perhaps."

The DCI was just about to argue, when the phone rang. "DCI Turner?"

He was on the phone for about a minute. Sienna, watched the changing expression on his face. His light-hearted smile from their conversation transformed to one of extreme seriousness as his brow furrowed.

"And you're sure that's the right address?" he asked the caller. "Okay, thanks, I don't want this going any further is that clear? Right, thanks."

He ended the call and looked at Sienna "What the fuck is going on here?" He asked her, not expecting an answer.

"What's happened?"

"That was forensics, they traced the IP address."

"And?" Sienna was on the edge of her seat.

"It's registered to a house on the edge of Highbridge. The address was checked with the landlord, and it's currently being let out to a Cheryl Markowska."

----o----

"I'm giving you one more chance to tell me the truth PC Andrews," DI Khatri was trying to get the officer's undivided attention now but, PC Andrews was lost for words. In fact, he was petrified.

Callum felt the situation was not as it might appear. He sat forward leaning on his knees with his elbows. "Dale, you do get how serious this is don't you? You're about to be arrested on suspicion of murder. You do get that, don't you?"

The PC concurred

"Now, tell us again the truth." Callum sat up. "Did you take the laptop straight to the IT forensic team? Or did you pass it to someone else to do it for you?"

PC Andrews put his face in his hands, pulling them back over his head. Looking down, he spoke quietly. "I just wanted to get back up to the incident room." He explained finally. "I get treated like the errand boy round here, I'm sick of it."

Callum already knew the answer to the next question but asked it anyway. "Right, so, you thought delivering the laptop to forensics was beneath you." The frustration in Callum's voice was clear to everyone in the room. "Did you give the laptop to somebody else?"

The PC dipped his head in confirmation, too nervous to speak.

DI Khatri spoke next. "Who did you give it too?"

PC Andrews sighed knowing there was no way he was getting out of this one, he looked up at them, resigned to his fate. He finally answered. "PC Markowska."

Chapter 30

PC Markowska arrived at work just before twelve. She walked in through the custody suite, past the Sergeants office towards Sienna's office. She knocked on Sienna's door and received no reply. Turning to look behind her, she turned back and went into the room and closed the door. Leafing through files on Sienna's desk, she jumped as the door suddenly opened. Callum walked in and stood in the door way.

"Sarg!" She started shakily, "I was just looking for a file for the investigation team." She lied.

"No problem, did you find it?"

"No, it must be upstairs."

"Probably. Can I have a word in my office?" Callum asked, casually.

"Of course Sarg." PC Markowska, followed him into his office.

As they entered the room, DI Khatri, who had been sitting at the sergeant's desk stood up as Callum closed the door behind them, positioning himself behind the officer.

"Cheryl Markowska, I'm arresting you on suspicion of the murders of Elaine Jackson and Emilie Wythe."

She said nothing, there was not even a flicker of reaction. She didn't protest, retaliate, or even cry. Her expression was stone like. Callum felt a chill rise up his spine.

DI Khatri continued the formalities of her arrest. Callum led her out into the custody suite, and the surrounding officers looked on in disbelief. After she was officially booked into custody, she was placed in a cell by Callum. By now, there were a crowd of officers there, all asking questions at once. Callum told them to get back to work, promising he would update them as soon as he could.

So it was done, they had their first suspect in custody. Only it didn't feel good. The fact one of their own had been arrested as an accomplice in the murders of two women, possibly more, was a bitter pill to swallow. One that would shock his colleagues to the core.

DCI Sloane was at his desk going through PC Markowska's file. She had transferred to Highbridge six weeks ago from Dorset after taking a month off on leave. She had an exemplary record. She was punctual and had good references from her previous station. There was nothing to suggest there was even a hint of the suspect they now held in custody.

Sienna was battling with herself. She had got the officer who she had liked wrong, so completely wrong. It had rocked her confidence and made her doubt everything she had provided the team with so far. Deep in her thoughts, Callum knocked on the frame of the open door.

"We've got Cheryl Markowska in custody." He looked down at Sienna, "She was in your office looking through your desk."

"How did she react?" Sienna croaked, her voice was dry. Callum noticed her tone and looked at her concerned.

"She didn't, Doc. She didn't even blink. It was eerie really. Are you okay?"

Sienna didn't answer, she nodded lightly and stood up, keeping her focus on the case, she spoke again. "She's resigned to her fate. It's the only way she knows. I'd like to sit in on the interview if I may?" Her question was directed at the DCI.

"I haven't got a problem with that." The DCI agreed.

Sienna walked to the door. Looking distracted, speaking over her shoulder she called out "I'll be in my office, let me know when you're ready."

Callum looked on perplexed between the door and the DCI. Noticing his concern, the DCI reassured him. "It's not you Cal. She's beating herself up for getting Cheryl wrong. She liked her and didn't see what was really there."

"But none of us did." Callum argued.

"I know, but it's the Doc's job to see these things. You and I both know she didn't see it because she had no reason to look. If she'd known from the beginning, or maybe, if we'd got that video sooner, then maybe she would have found it."

"So what do I do? She's been through enough the last few days."

"Just leave it. As much as I love that girl, she hates being wrong about anything, she'll berate herself, lick her wounds and bounce back. She always bounces back." DCI Sloane confirmed.

Callum nodded, but he was still worried. The DCI could both see and understand his concern.

"Cal, how much has Doc told you about her past?"

"Not a lot to be honest. I know she was in care and she had a bad marriage and divorce. She didn't go into details and I didn't want to push her."

The DCI told Callum to close the door and sit back down.

"This is really up to her to tell you, but I'll give you the highlights. Sienna originally became a Criminal Psychologist to try and understand her own father. When Sienna was eight, her old man was convicted for the rape and murder of twelve prostitutes. When he wasn't out killing, he was at home beating her and her mother black and blue. After his conviction, her mother committed suicide. That's why she was in care. She survived that, then married a man who had endless affairs and carried on with the beatings she'd got as a child. Doc's real maiden name is Lane. When she got divorced she had it changed by deed poll to Turner. She didn't want her married name, or her father's name."

Callum was mortified, his heart was breaking for Sienna and the suffering she must have gone through throughout her life. "I had no idea it was that bad."

"The thing is," The DCI added "she survived all that and a lot more. It's made her as hard as nails. The only thing that scares that girl is her own heart. She'll get over this and she'll move on. She always has and she always will."

Callum remembered the things he had said to her when they argued about being closed off. Now he fully understood why she was so distant. Only, it didn't make him want to trust that she was strong enough to get through this alone. Instead, it made him feel even more protective. All he wanted to do now was shield her from the world so she could depend on someone else for a change.

"Thanks for filling me in, Sir. I know it goes without saying that I let Si tell me this in her own time."

"Agreed." The DCI nodded, "And for fuck sake, it's Terry or Guv. I think we're beyond formalities now your courting my surrogate daughter, don't you?" He laughed attempting to lighten the mood.

Callum nodded laughing, "Better not let her hear you use the term 'courting', she'll have forty fits, Guv."

Terry pulled a feigned terrified face as he shook Callum's hand. "Fuck that, I'm not brave enough." He laughed.

Finishing their conversation, the DCI left to interview Cheryl Markowska.

Callum stayed behind, going over everything he had learned in his head, until he received a call to assist another officer.

Chapter 31

Cheryl Markowska sat opposite DCI Sloane and Sienna looking drained and defeated. The only time she had spoken was to decline a solicitor. They had been sitting with her for over an hour and she had not uttered a word.

Accepting he was getting nowhere, the DCI looked at Sienna and prompted her to speak to Cheryl. Sienna knew Cheryl was completely shut down. She needed to bring her back, no matter what it took, or they would get nowhere. It would be only a matter of time before the dominant suspect killed again. They had to get a lead on him, fast.

"Cheryl, when I arrived at Elaine's house, do you remember? The day I found the bloody underwear. Did you put it there?"

Cheryl, who had kept her head down until now, lifted her head slightly and stared at Sienna.

"Who told you to put them there Cheryl?"

Still nothing.

"What about the mobile phone posted to my home?" Sienna leant forward to study Cheryl's eyes.

"You came to my house that day, along with DCI Sloane and DI Khatri. You even hugged me."

Cheryl was looking up now, her nostrils were flaring slightly as her breathing quickened.

"I remember you could barely speak, I had to get you a drink. Watching that footage was bad enough, but you had to watch it in person didn't you, and that was too much, wasn't it?"

Sienna could see she was agitating Cheryl, but she needed her to react. "Having to watch that poor, young, defenceless girl being brutally tortured like that while she pleaded with you to help her. Yet you did nothing, you just stood there and let it happen."

Sienna tilted her head, "Were you scared?" Sienna's eyes narrowed, "Or have I got it completely wrong, did you enjoy watching? Maybe you even joined in. Did it excite you, seeing her beg and plead for mercy as the knife sliced into her body, over and over again?"

Leaning in closer still, Sienna fired her final shot, "In fact, maybe you instigated the whole thing. Maybe, he was playing out a fantasy to please you. That's it, isn't it? You're the monster."

Cheryl was up out of her seat at lightning speed. She swung her fist at Sienna across the table hitting Sienna in her right eye, before lunging at her again, scratching Sienna's jaw as she tried to reach her. The DCI hit the alarm band and grabbed her, pinning her to the wall.

"You think I wanted that? You haven't got a fucking clue. His reach is long."

Dave Fletcher and another officer flew in to the room. Cheryl started to sob. "I couldn't stop him, there was nothing I could do. I'm sorry." She kept repeating she was sorry, as the sergeant took her away.

The DCI went over to Sienna, he lifted her chin tilting her head to one side. "You're gonna have a bit of a shiner there, Doc."

Sienna agreed, "I've had worse."

"Did you get the reaction you wanted?"

"I did."

"Feel better now?" The DCI asked.

"A bit." Her voice was like steel as she answered.

As they walked to the stairs and the DCI added, "You know Cal's gonna flip, don't you?"

"Uh-huh!" She agreed flippantly.

"Poor bloke, has got no idea what he's taking on with you does he?"

Sienna didn't respond.

----o----

Callum walked into the incident room and stormed over to Sienna who, was sitting on the table at the far side of the room. He tilted her chin to look at her face. Her eye was slightly swollen and, had already started to bruise.

"I just got back from a call. Dave told me what happened? Are you ok?"

Sienna put her hand over his, "I'm fine Cal honest, hazard of the job." She smiled.

Cal objected, "No Si, it's not. You shouldn't have been in there, god knows what she's capable of. She's a killer, don't you get that?"

Sienna had a feeling he was going to react like this, but even so it still irritated her. "Actually Callum, this" she emphasised, pointing to her eye, "is part of my job. Besides," she added sarcastically, "She hit me in the face, it's not as if she charged at me with a flame thrower. I think you're over reacting."

Callum bit back, "You're not a one woman fucking army, Sienna. Stop being so bloody obstinate. Okay, so it was one punch but what next? Where does it end? You've already got this freak stalking you. I defended you to stay on this case, but this has to stop."

Behind them, the room started to fill. The DCI had organised another briefing. "Look," Sienna insisted pointedly, trying to avoid the others in the room from hearing, "can we discuss this later?"

"OK, later then." He agreed before adding "But we will discuss it Sienna."

Sienna was seething but she was unable to retaliate as the DCI was now calling for everyone's attention.

"If I can have some quiet please, we've had some important developments in the case." He looked round making sure everyone was quiet.

"As you've all heard by now, at midday today PC Cheryl Markowska was arrested on suspicion of the murder of Elaine Jackson and Emilie Wythe."

The DCI elaborated the whole story of how they traced the IP address back to her, the wiped laptop through to the interview and the attack on Sienna in the interview room.

The Chief Superintendent was also in the room and was the first to speak after the DCI had delivered the update. "Are you telling me you actually think Cheryl Markowska is the instigator of these murders?"

He was clearly worried, after all, this could be detrimental to his plans to expand Highbridge as a serious crime unit.

Sienna, recognising the need to placate him, "Not at all. In fact, totally the opposite. Cheryl hasn't got a harmful bone in her body."

"Doc!" Callum called out in disbelief, "She just punched you in the face. How is that not harmful?"

Trying hard to keep her composure, Sienna argued, "In the first place, she was full of remorse the second she lashed out. Reacting like that was totally out of character for her."

The Chief Superintendent interrupted, "And in the second place?"

"In the second place, I intentionally instigated her outburst."

"You what?" Callum was on his feet, rubbing the back of his neck, he was livid. "You encouraged her to attack you?"

"She had completely withdrawn, it was the only of getting her to reconnect. It's only a matter of time before there is another murder and we don't have time to wait for her to come around on her own."

Seeing the need to diffuse the situation before somebody self-combusted, the DCI interjected. "Look let's bring this all back a notch. Sienna is right, we were getting nowhere, so the Doc took one for the team. If you want to blame anyone, blame me. I knew what she was doing, but I underestimated how fast Markowska would move."

The Chief Superintendent was bewildered about the entire conversation on front of him. "That was very brave of you to make such a sacrifice Dr Turner. It goes without saying that you always go above and beyond, and are outstanding in your field of expertise. However, in future, I think it may be wise to ensure stringent precautions are taken."

Sienna consented gratefully. He had never been her favourite person but, she appreciated the Superintendent mediating so they could stay focused on the investigation.

"Now that's settled, where do we go from here?" He asked.

"I go back in." Sienna declared with conviction.

Callum was on his feet again. "You're crazy!"

Trying to remain professional, Sienna explained. "Cheryl has snapped herself back to reality. The fact she was so remorseful about hurting me, shows she feels some sort of connection with me. I strongly believe I have a better chance of getting her to open up than anyone else."

The Chief Superintendent, stroked his chin, then nodding, he turned to the DCI, "What's your opinion Terry?"

"The Doc's right sir, I tried for over an hour and couldn't even get Markowska to blink." As he spoke, he looked at Callum who by now was fit to explode. "We go back in but have PC Mitchell, sit next to Markowska, I'll be there too, so Doc won't be in any danger."

"Okay, we'll go with it. Keep me informed please." The Chief Superintendent went to walk from the room but turned back and spoke to Callum "Have PC Andrews sent up to my office in the meantime please, Sergeant Blake. After today, I don't want that fool stepping a foot back in my station."

Callum concurred, "Yes, Sir."

"Oh, and Sergeant Blake?" He walked over to Callum, speaking to him quietly. "A word to the wise, Dr Turner, is a law unto herself. She may sometimes flaunt procedure, but she does it for good reason. Which is why, I am willing to turn the odd blind eye. You have more chance of turning water into glass, than changing her, and it would be foolhardy to try."

"Thank you, Sir." Callum replied, but he had no intention of taking his advice.

He walked over and took Sienna by the elbow leading her to the far corner of the room, "Sienna, you can't go back in there, how many more risks are you prepared to take?"

Sienna turned to face him, folding her arms she continued, "There is a maniac out there and we're running out of time. If I have to take a punch in the eye to prevent another woman enduring that monster's torture, then so be it. Besides, you really are overreacting."

He was worried about her, but he was also angry. "We all want to get this bloke, please just stop being so bloody stubborn. It won't kill you to let people protect you now and then."

"Look, I've been doing this alone for far too long to let anyone wrap me up in cotton wool and put me up on a bloody pedestal." Before walking off, she added, "Callum, I'm not going to change, this is more than my job, and I refuse to be any different. If you can't accept that, then maybe we need to walk away from each other now."

"Yeah, maybe we do!" he called after her.

Chapter 32

Sienna sat next to the DCI, with PC Mitchell sitting next to Cheryl Markowska.

She leant forward and looked directly into Cheryl's eyes. "Cheryl, I know you are not capable of carrying out the killings of Elaine and Emilie. But I also know you are protecting the person who did."

Cheryl looked up at Sienna, noticing her eye. Sienna could see the remorse on her face.

"You've been controlled by this man for so long, you don't know how to function without him. The hold he has over you, the fear he has instilled in you. I understand why you're so scared." She leant forward and covered Cheryl's hands with hers speaking reassuringly,

"We can protect you."

"But that's just it, you don't understand, you can't protect me, nobody can."

"So help me Cheryl. Help me to understand."

"I'm sorry, it doesn't matter what you do, any of you. He'll get to me. He gets everywhere."

Sienna decided to try a different tact.

"Okay, so can you at least tell me how long ago you met him? Was it when you worked in Dorset?"

Cheryl didn't answer.

"You weren't at Dorset when I was consulting there were you?"

"No, I arrived after you left. I was only there for a month."

"You arrived here just after me, too didn't you?"

Cheryl nodded.

"Where did you go between leaving Dorset and coming here?"

She didn't answer.

"Did you have a break? A holiday maybe?"

"No."

"Did you travel?"

"No."

"Were you sick?"

"No."

Sienna leaned in closer to Cheryl, speaking softer this time.

"You tried to run, didn't you?"

Cheryl dropped her head to the floor. Reaching out. Sienna gently lifted her chin so she had to look at her.

"You tried to run, didn't you?"

Tears filled Cheryl's eyes, she blinked tightly as they stung her eyes.

"You tried to run but he found you, didn't he?"

This time Cheryl broke down. Nodding as she spoke,

"He'll always find me. I want to help you but I can't. I'm so sorry for all those girls, and I'm so sorry I hit you. But please, I can't tell you who he is. "She put her head back down, wracking sobs left her body. She repeated what she said earlier, "His reach is long, far too long."

Sienna looked at the DCI and shook her head. Cheryl was terrified, there was no way she would give up her controller. Whatever hold he had over her, it was too strong.

"Okay Cheryl, I think it's time you had a break."

She patted Cheryl's hand. You'll have to go back to the cell, but I'll ask them to organise some food and a cup of tea for you."

The DCI suspended the interview and they left the room.

"So what do you think, Doc?" The DCI asked as they made their way up the stairs.

"We need to go to Dorset, the answer's there I would bet my life on it." The pair stopped on the stairs so Sienna could explain.

"I think it's a bit more than a coincidence that we both worked out of the same station, then she arrives here after me."

"I agree," He fell silent wondering how to broach the next subject without her going off the deep end. "Look Doc, I need you to hear me out on this one. If he is coming after you, I think it might me an idea to get you away for a while."

"You're not pulling me off this case, Terry. Look what happened the last time when I was pulled from the investigation in Dorset."

"Doc, I'm not pulling you from the case, I think you should go to Dorset and speak to your old colleagues, see what you can find out about Cheryl's contacts down there."

Accepting the DCI was right, she added, "There's something else though Terry."

Interested, the DCI tilted his head, and narrowed his eyes, "Go on?"

"Cheryl repeated the same thing twice, 'His reach is too long'."

"And?"

"And, she's safe in the custody of a Police Station, surrounded by officers. Yet, she still believes he can get to her."

The realisation hit the DCI like a freight train. "He's on the force."

"Exactly."

As they were speaking, DI Khatri was passing them on the stairs. The DCI turned to him. "Baz, can you get someone to run the Doc home? She's going down to Dorset tomorrow to speak with Cheryl's colleagues. Also, I want a car outside her house tonight." He turned to Sienna, "I know Callum's there, but I'm not taking any chances."

Thinking Callum would now be the last person she'd be seeing again, she agreed. "That's fine, I'll get a bag ready and head down there first thing in the morning."

Baz, when you get back I'd like to see you and Callum in my office.

Chapter 33

Callum was in the yard outside the custody suite, pacing up and down, running his hands through his hair. Dave Fletcher, came out to check on him. "How's your lady after her rumble? She ok?" He already knew what had happened between them, but he wanted Callum to open up under his own volition.

"Oh, yeah she's ok mate." He turned throwing his hands up in the air. "In fact, she's so fucking perfect, she doesn't need me for anything." He yelled across the yard.

"Mate, calm the fuck down. That woman loves the bones of you."

The word 'love' had never been mentioned before and it stopped Callum in his tracks. It was a word that used to send him screaming for the hills. Until now. This time he didn't want to run. Only it was too late. They were done. "She's got a funny way of showing it ain't she?"

"Why?" Dave laughed, "Because she won't let you play the white knight every time she lands in hot water?" Feeling frustrated at his best mate, he decided he needed a few home truths. "For fuck sake Cal, you're my best mate, and I'd kill for you, you know that. But wake up and smell the shit your shovelling over yourself will you."

Callum was shocked. Dave had always been honest but this was an eye opener. "You been taking lessons off the Doc or something." Callum joked, calming himself down.

Dave laughed, "Seriously mate, if she was the girly, weak bird you want her to be, you'd be bored in a minute and you know it. You can't have it all. You either need to accept who she is and buckle up your safety harness or walk away."

Callum agreed sadly, "It's too late now anyway mate. I've fucked up, she won't wanna know now."

As he spoke, PC Andrews stepped out from the doorway having heard the last part of the conversation. He had just been suspended pending investigation and a recommendation that he is permanently dismissed from the force. He didn't have a lot to lose.

"Ah, what's up?" he sneered. "Trouble in paradise? Don't worry, you send her round to me, I'll give her a good sorting for ya."

Before he could take another step, Callum was on him. Grabbing him by his collar, he slammed him up against the brick wall, raising his arm with his fist clenched. Dave grabbed him and struggled to pull him back. Finally getting him off Andrews, he turned and grabbed him, himself.

"Listen to me you snivelling little scrote. You're nothing but a dickless streak of piss. Now fuck off, and stay fucked off! If I ever, hear you speak about the Doc like that again, I'll rip off your arm and beat you to death with it!"

With that, Dave threw Andrews to the floor. Andrews, scrabbled to his feet and ran to the gate. Away from the reach of the two sergeants, Andrews decided to try his luck some more. "You're nothing but a bunch of wankers, fuck you, and fuck this place." Dave, and Callum turned to walk towards him and Andrews fled.

The pair were laughing now. Dave put his hand on Callum's shoulder. "Don't worry about that gobby little bastard, the only way he'd ever get laid is to crawl up a chicken's arse and wait."

Callum doubled over in laughter. Dave Fletcher's way with words was infamous.

Returning to their conversation before the interruption, Dave spoke again. "Cal, it's never too late. My misses had me jumping through hoops, shit, she still does. Nothing worth having, was ever achieved easily."

Callum patted him on the shoulder, "I hope so, thanks mate."

As Callum walked off, Dave called behind him, mimicking a ten-year-old school boy. "Callum's in lurrve!"

Not looking back, Callum raised his hand up behind him and extended his middle finger. "Fuck off, Dave."

----0----

DI Khatri was already in the DCI's office when Callum arrived.

"Nice of you to join us Sergeant Blake."

"Sorry Guv, I was just,"

"Just calming down I hope," the DCI interrupted.

Callum didn't react. Looking round the office as if Sienna might be hiding under a chair, he enquired, "Where's Doc?"

"Gone home, and before you fly off again, she's got an officer outside the apartment."

Callum's face reddened.

"Don't worry, you'll be joining her shortly. I've cleared it with the Chief Inspector, I want you to accompany the Doc to Dorset. Bit of fact finding if you will."

Callum looked bewildered as the DCI offered him a seat to explain.

Chapter 34

Sienna had spent the last forty minutes standing in the shower. The build-up of emotion from the day had got to her, and behind the safety of closed doors, she finally let go. Heaving sobs left her body as she stood in the steaming cubicle, allowing the hot water envelope her. She sobbed for the victims, who had been brutally tortured and slaughtered. She sobbed for Cheryl, whose life was ruined and would never return to any kind of normality. She sobbed for the threat that veiled her by the suspect, who was nowhere near being caught. Finally, most of all she sobbed for Callum.

She knew they had both said things that could not be taken back, their parting words spelled the end of their brief but powerful relationship. She felt like her whole world was suddenly caving in on her.

When she had nothing left to give, she stepped out of the shower, dried herself off, and slipped into her robe. She packed a weekend bag ready for the trip to Dorset and booked a bed and breakfast.

Still upset, Sienna got up from the sofa, went to the kitchen, and tiptoed to reach a glass from the cupboard. She needed a drink. She actually wanted several, but she had to keep a clear head for the next day.

Sitting back down with a large glass of merlot, there was a knock at the door. A trickle of fear ran down her spine. She walked to the window and looked down. Seeing the officer was still there in his car, she felt a little easier. She turned her music down and went to the door, looking through the spy hole, she saw Callum standing there. Her heart picked up a pace, and she could feel her legs shaking. She really wasn't ready to see him yet. Believing their parting words earlier were final, the last thing she needed was another lecture. Composing herself as much as she could, she opened the door.

Callum, stood awkwardly with his head to one side, rubbing the back of his head with one hand. He smiled anxiously, "Can I come in?" He begged, hoping she wouldn't slam the door in his face.

Without speaking, Sienna stepped to the side, presenting an outstretched arm directing him in.

With her voice breaking, Sienna asked "What can I do for you?" She was trembling, desperately trying to hold her nerve.

"I've just come from the DCI. He wants me to come with you to Dorset tomorrow. I just wanted to let you know, if it's a problem, I can get Dave to go with you."

Thinking that Callum was trying to get out of going, she replied haughtily, "If that's what you want, fine!"

Callum stepped forward, he couldn't leave it, "No, Si that's not what I want at all." He lowered his tone, his voice was trembling, and he felt as if he'd been shot.

"I know I've blown it with you, I just don't want to cause you any discomfort."

Sienna could see the pain in his eyes now. Her shoulders dropped, as she stepped towards him, "Cal, you haven't blown it," She paused, still protecting herself a little, "unless… unless that's what you want?"

"God, Si, that's the last thing I want." He moved closer, gently running his fingers down her arm and taking her hand.

"I don't want that either." She reassured. "We do need to talk though."

She led him to the couch and they sat down facing each other. Callum reached out his hand, cupping her face gently. She took his hand, kissing the palm. Callum was lost to her, and he knew it, he had to tell her.

"Si, I'm so sorry about the way I behaved. I know I was wrong and I know I was smothering you. When I first met you, you interested me so much, you were like no one I had ever met before." As he spoke his heart was beating so fast, he thought it was going to explode inside him. He pushed himself forward, knowing he had to get his words out.

"I knew I had to get to know you more. The more I got to know you, the more I couldn't stop thinking about you, and now, you're in my every waking thoughts. I even dream about you. It's like you've consumed me. I feel like I'm drowning only, I don't want to get out of the water. When you're not there, I can't function properly, I can't think, I'm a wreck."

Sienna interrupted, "Would you like me to back off, Cal. I'd understand if,"

"No! Oh god, no. Si, I never want that believe me. It's just the opposite. I want to be in your life and I want you in mine. One hundred percent, not playing cat and mouse games with each other. I want you in every part of my life."

A tear ran down Sienna's cheek and Callum moved towards her kissing it away. He took a breath and held her head tenderly in his hands.

"Si, I love you, I'm in love with everything about you. I love your beautiful face, your sense of humour, the way you pick on me, I love your figure, your strength, your passion when you fight for what you believe in, I even love your pig-headed stubbornness and sarcasm."

Sienna was crying silently now, as tears flowed down her cheeks. She felt the same and, she couldn't deny it any longer even if she tried, and she didn't want to.

"She kissed him, deeply, passionately, with every fibre of her being." Tearing herself away, she stared in to his smouldering blue eyes. "Cal, I love you too, I love you more, than I ever thought I could love someone. But, you have to let me be me. You fell for me because I'm a fighter, because I'm pig-headed and stubborn."

"Oh, so you admit it then?" He smiled, kissing her tear stained cheeks.

She playfully slapped his shoulder. "Shut up!" She laughed. "But, honestly Cal, if I was a needy woman screaming at you from the stairwell, you wouldn't have given me a second glance. Please don't try to turn me into her." She pleaded.

Callum leant forward and kissed her again before he answered. "I won't, I promise, but you need to learn when to drop the stubbornness. You have to promise me, if you ever feel out of your depth, if you ever need me, you tell me ok? In the meantime, I'll trust that you are more than capable of taking care of yourself."

He was right and, Sienna knew he was right. "I promise I will."

Callum pulled her into his arms, her robe falling lose at her sides, "I swear to you, I have never felt like this about anyone in my entire life. You've completely and utterly, blown my mind."

He stood up and pulled her into him, he could feel her bare skin through his clothes. He bent his head towards her, placing his hand on the crook of her neck, he kissed her hard, his tongue probing every part of her mouth, Sienna, feeling as if she had turned to putty, moaning with pleasure as she responded to his searching tongue, fumbling at the buttons of his shirt, undoing each one before reaching up, pulling the shirt down over his smooth, broad shoulders.

Pulling her back in, Callum groaned, as he felt her naked breasts up against his skin. He stooped down and picked her up and she wrapped her legs around his waist. He could feel the power of his own blood, rushing through his veins, his heart was pumping hard, as he felt the warmth between her legs, against his stomach. He carried Sienna through to the bedroom, all the time kissing her. Laying her back on the bed, he assessed her, running his large hands down from her neck over her firm breasts, down to her navel, and inner thighs. She arched her back moaning in ecstasy.

"Si, you're so beautiful, I love you so much." He lowered himself down on to her gently, kissing her neck while Sienna stroked her nails lightly down his toned back with one hand, using the other to unbuckle his belt, his button, and his zip. She wanted him desperately.

Callum paused to finish undressing, all the time watching her firm curvy body. He lowered himself back down to her. He kissed down her body, circling her erect nipples with his tongue, gently nibbling her, delighting at the silkiness of her skin, making his way down to her navel, sending electricity through Sienna's body every time he made contact with her skin. Biting her bottom lip, she threw her head back arching as she did, calling out in a state of delirium, as he moved between her legs, exploring her soft moist folds with his tongue, pushing his fingers inside her, feeling the warm, smooth, tightness of what was to come.

He brought her to an earth-shattering climax as she screamed out, her arms outstretched to her sides, fingers digging into the sheets. He pulled himself upwards, running his hand down her body, stopping between her legs, while he watched her. Savouring the erotic beauty on her face in delicious wonder as he worked her through the remainder of her orgasm.

When she was sated, he kissed her eyes, her cheeks, and her mouth, lifting his head, he gently stroked her face, resting his hand on her neck, staring at her lovingly as he entered her. Throwing his head up from the intense pleasure as her hot, wet, tightness gripped him, pulling him in deeper, he pushed into her slowly, deeply, fighting to keep control. Sienna, matched him, pushing into him with every stroke, each time electrifying him with increasing intensity until, he could not hold on any longer. She could feel him swell as he was about to come, pushing into her deeper, faster, she pushed her hips up to meet him, her nails digging into his back, biting her lip, reacting to the sheer force of him. Snapping his head back, Callum erupted, crying out as he did. The power she had given him, coming to an explosive end.

Callum's arms buckled as Sienna clung to him, both breathless. Beads of sweat ran down the centre of Callum's back. They lay together, holding each other as if they might be torn apart.

Recovering slightly, Callum propped himself up on one elbow and swept a dark ringlet of hair away from her face, he kissed her slowly, small loving kisses, as he whispered how much he loved her.

They spent the rest of the night in each other's arms. Caressing each other's bodies, making love three more times before finally falling to sleep. Callum's body was wrapped around Sienna protectively. Both knowing that whatever happened, they would never let each other go again.

Sienna opened her eyes, to meet Callum's handsome, smiling face staring down at her. Propped up on his elbow with his hand resting on her stomach.

"Morning gorgeous!" He greeted, bending to kiss her.

She smiled, closing her eyes, and slowly opening them again as if she thought she was dreaming. "How long have you been watching me?" She asked quizzically with one eye brow raised.

Callum looked at his watch. "Only about an hour, eleven minutes and sixteen seconds." He smirked shyly.

Sienna reached out her hand and searched for her phone. She picked it up looking at her reflection in the blank screen.

"What's wrong?" He questioned.

"I'm just checking you haven't drawn a moustache on my face." She joked.

"That's not fair, I wouldn't do that to you." He exclaimed in feigned shock. "Besides, I couldn't find a pen."

Sienna slapped him, "Don't even think about it."

"As if! It's more than my life's worth."

"Hey!" She squealed. "I'm not that scary." Knowing full well, she probably was.

Callum's phone vibrated from the bedside table, he leant over her, stopping to kiss her as he did. Straightening, he read the text and blushed, making Sienna curious. "What is it?" She questioned.

"It's a text from Dave." He replied awkwardly.

"Dave makes you blush?" Raising one eyebrow, she added, "Anything you care to tell me about you two? I mean, if I have competition,"

He turned, tickling her as she squealed in shock. "Very funny, Miss."

"So, come on, you've captured my interest Sergeant Blake, why does Dave make you blush like a schoolgirl."

Callum took a deep breath, handing her the phone. "Please don't be angry, I was a mess thinking I'd lost you. I needed to talk to somebody, and I can trust him with my life."

Sienna read the text, and a wry smile spread across her lips.

Did you speak to Doc?
Did you sort things out with her,
or bottle out and abort mission?
Man up you Twat!

"Ah, so you got the 'home truth' lecture."

"Yeah, he basically told me if I didn't get my act together, I was going to lose you. I couldn't handle that."

Sienna pulled her to him and kissed him. "Well I'm glad you listened to him."

Sienna looked at him with a sly grin, she went back to Callum's phone and typed, then pressed send.

He had to wrestle her for the phone, finally getting her to free it by tickling her some more. He opened the screen to read it and burst out laughing.

The Eagle has landed!

"You do know you're completely crazy don't you Dr Turner."

"Uhuh! It's one of the things you love about me."

He couldn't argue with that.

Sienna went to sit up, "Coffee?"

Callum pushed her back down to the bed, "Not so fast Dr Turner. We've got more important matters to attend to." He ran his hand down Sienna's body, taking in her naked beauty with his eyes. He scooped her up, rolling her on top of him. She leant in to kiss him, their fingers interlocked above Callum's head. Gently biting at his neck and chest, she slid her body down, gasping as she lowered her hips onto him. She made love to him deep and slow, gripping around his hardness moving her hips in rhythm, making him groan with each deep thrust, working faster and faster as she could feel him losing control. He grabbed her hips and pushed his pelvis up, gasping loudly as he released the pressure of her lovemaking inside her, his fingers digging into her hips as he lost control, shuddering over and over as his orgasm reached a crescendo.

She lowered herself down lying to the side of him, kissing his neck as he clung to her, fighting to regain control of his breathing.

"Don't ever leave me Si, I'm totally lost to you, you know that, don't you?"

Sienna knew he meant it, she could never remember feeling so secure, so loved, so craved for, and she felt the same about him. She propped herself up on her elbow, tracing his face with her finger, as he closed his eyes enjoying her touch.

"Cal, I can't imagine a life without you in it now." She responded seriously.

He opened his eyes and looked at her lovingly, he was drowning from the love he felt for her. She laid to the side of him and he pulled her close, his hand on her neck, stroking her face. His mind went back to everything the DCI had told him about her past and he ached at the thought of what she had been through. "I promise, I'll never hurt you, I'd lay down my life for you."

"I know." She smiled.

They lay cuddling for the next hour before finally getting up. Sienna was in the shower, while Callum made coffee, before joining her. They lathered and washed each other's bodies, exploring every inch of each other, before he lifted her up, wrapping her legs around his waist, making love to her again, as the water flowed over their bodies.

It was ten o clock before they had finally managed to pull themselves away from one another long enough to get dressed. Stopping at Callum's for him to pack a weekend bag, they headed out to tell the officer on duty, he was okay to leave.

They argued all the way downstairs over who was driving, Callum teasing her about women drivers. Sienna finally telling him to shut up and drive. They headed to Callum's car to make their way to Dorset. It was not until they were half way down the M3, that Callum realised, he'd just won an argument. Not that he was brave enough to point that out of course. One thing he'd learned with Sienna was to quit while he was ahead.

Chapter 35

Kissing her mum goodbye and promising she would call in to see her the next day after work, PC Claire Mitchell skipped happily out of the front door and headed down Westfield Road. She was in a great mood and everything in her life was falling neatly into place. She had just rented a new flat, and nearly had enough money to buy herself a little run around to get her from A to B. She was enjoying her job, having only recently started at Highbridge, as a probationary police officer, she was throwing herself into her new role and relishing every minute of it.

The only blot on her landscape was the shocking arrest of her colleague yesterday. Even though, Cheryl Markowska, was being held for her part in the killings of two women, Claire could not help but feel sorry for her. Having been asked to sit in on the interview the previous day, she could tell how scared she was. She struggled to imagine anyone having that power over somebody.

However, she was pleased to have seen Dr Turner at work. The way she was willing to get hit in the face to get a result was awe inspiring. She planned on speaking to her when the case was over, to see if she could work alongside her more in the future, feeling she could learn a lot from her potential mentor.

Deciding to treat herself to some retail therapy, she headed for the High Street. It was her first day off in two weeks and with all the extra overtime, she thought she'd treat herself to a new 'power suit', just in case she was ever asked to work alongside CID in civvies. Being taken seriously, as a valued and respected colleague was important to her if she wanted to succeed. Her keenness and ambition flowed through her as naturally as her own life blood.

Eager to get to the shops, she took a short cut down Acer Avenue. Old run down factories, loomed over her on each side of the road which, were boarded up for demolition. Her mind filled with dreams of the future, she was oblivious to the world around her. So oblivious, she didn't notice the red car, parked up ahead of her.

Unknowingly, walking towards the vehicle, she was trying to decide, whether to go for a grey or black trouser suit. By the time she had registered the red Golf in front of her, the door had opened and a man was stepping out of the car. He straightened and faced her as she almost bumped into him. She was close enough to see the large open pores and red spider veins on his face caused by too much whisky. She was close enough to smell the abhorrent staleness of his breath. He tilted his head to one side and spoke. "I wonder if you'd be so kind as to pass on a message for Dr Turner for me?"

By the time she had processed all this information, she realised, she was too close.

Chapter 36

The old Dorset police station was a far cry from the more modern buildings of Highbridge. Originally an old court house, its architecture combined with old oak frames and the light musty smell which had ingrained itself into the walls over the years, only added to its character. On driving up to the impressive building, Sienna pointed out the fire damaged annex, which had been built in later years and provided a home for the administration and records offices.

Sienna and Callum were met at the front office which was smaller than the one at Highbridge, by an old colleague of Sienna's. Sienna had phoned ahead the day before and spoken to her. She had not explained in detail her reason for visiting, just that they wanted to discuss the case in more detail.

"Joyce, hi, it's so good to see you again." Sienna greeted the old colleague with warmth which was reciprocated in turn.

"Joyce, this is Sergeant Callum Blake from Highbridge Police Station. We have been working together on this case. Callum, this is DI Joyce Pembury. We worked together at length before I was taken off the case at this end."

"Against my advice, I might add." DI Pembury interjected, outstretching her arm she shook Callum's hand so hard, he had to flex his fingers when she had finally released her iron grip. "and, it's DCI Pembury now by the way," she corrected warmly, "but Joyce is just fine."

Raising her eyebrows to show her approval, Sienna congratulated the new DCI. "I'm impressed, when did that happen?"

"After you left, the report you left with me about PC Carter escalated. I persuaded her to make it official, an investigation was conducted, resulting in several female officers crawling out of the woodwork to make similar complaints."

Sienna turned to Callum to briefly explain. "PC Carter came to me for advice alleging the old DCI, 'DCI Doyle' was sexually harassing her."

"No allegedly about it as it turned out." DCI Pembury added, as if to highlight the scandal of it all. "He was, shall we say, 'asked' to retire, and I was offered the DCI position." She smiled, "Would've been rude to say no really." She roared, snorting as she laughed.

Pleasantries out of the way, Sienna steered the conversation back to the case. "As you know, Joyce, we've been trying to obtaining information regarding a case I'm consulting on in Highbridge regarding two murdered girls. There are many similarities with the "Woodland murders."

Joyce nodded in agreement, "Well, from what you've explained on the phone, it certainly seems the case. However, as we've previously told your colleagues at Highbridge, we suffered a great deal of damage following an arson attack on the station. I'm sure you saw the damage for yourself on the way in."

"We did." Callum agreed, "Looks nasty, nobody hurt I hope?" he enquired.

"No, thank heavens but, the records, evidence, and communications rooms were completely destroyed. We managed to salvage the back-up tapes etcetera, but the information was limited. We've already sent you everything we had I'm afraid."

Joyce was now leading them along the corridor to her office. "Please, take a seat, I'll arrange some coffee."

Joyce walked out of the room to organise refreshments and Callum leaned over in his chair to Sienna. "Shit, she's scarier than you." He mocked.

Sienna giggled quietly, "I know, she's as large as life, but her heart is where it should be, and she gets the job done."

Joyce bustled back in with a tray, containing three steaming mugs of coffee, milk, and sugar. Setting the tray down she passed a mug to each of them, telling them to help themselves to milk and sugar.

When they were all settled, Sienna raised the subject again. "The thing is Joyce, we've had a recent development which relates directly to Dorset. The problem is, it's sensitive. I was hoping we could run it by you in confidence and get your thoughts."

"Well, as you know Doc, I'm nothing if not sensitive." She winked and the irony was not lost on anyone in the room. She got up and closed the door to her office, then turning to sit back down again. "You'd better fill me in then."

They spent the next half an hour relaying the whole case from the start. Finding the burnt corpse of Elaine Jackson, the underwear from the last victim found in Dorset, the mobile phone footage sent to Sienna's home, to the arrest of PC Cheryl Markowska and her comment about the suspect having a long reach.

When they finished, Joyce scratched her temple, closing her eyes tightly. "I remember PC Markowska well, in the brief time she was here. She had transferred here because she had moved in with her boyfriend who apparently lived in Dorset. She was a very quiet individual, good at her job but quiet all the same. In fact, we were sorry to lose her."

"Do you know who her partner was?" Callum queried.

"No, she never really spoke about him." Pausing for recollection, she added, "She played her cards close to her chest that one. Just got on with the job, until she suddenly upped and left us that is."

Sienna straightened in her chair, "What do you mean, suddenly?"

"Exactly that. She called in and spoke to the Chief Inspector. Informed him her mum was ill and she had to go and look after her long term. When we heard she had transferred to Highbridge later down the line, we just assumed her mother had died or something so she went back to work."

"Did she work on the Woodlands case at all after I left." Sienna asked.

"Yes, as I remember, she did. Doyle drafted her in, right after she started here, actually." She sat up, pointing her stout manicured finger in the air. "Actually, I remember wondering shortly after, if she was one of Doyle's potential 'protégés', as it was around the time evidence was being gathered on him."

Sitting forward in her seat, Sienna looked from Joyce to Callum, as if a light bulb went on in her head. "I notice, CID has moved downstairs now"

Joyce looked a little confused at the question, which was completely off the subject, but replied anyway. "Since the fire, the powers that be decided to downsize the station. We'll eventually be incorporated to the main station in Poole. The first floor is no longer used."

"I see. Is DCI Doyle's old office still up there?"

"Yes, it is. Desk and everything." She squinted looking at Sienna. "What's going on in that large brain of yours Doc? I remember that look."

"I'm not sure yet. It may be nothing but, may I see his office please? If you have time that is."

"Always have time for you, Doc." She smiled honestly. "Come on, no time like the present." She stood up and led them out up the stairs to the old offices.

In the old stuffy office, Sienna was taken back to the times she stood in there arguing with the overbearing, oppressive DCI who would listen to nobody, especially female colleagues. Sienna had tried on many occasion and despite getting the measure of him, she had exhausted herself in the fight.

Walking around the office, she stood looking at the desk for a brief moment. Callum and Joyce were watching her curiously.

"What is it, Doc?" Callum asked.

"I'm not entirely sure to be honest, Cal. I just can't get Cheryl's comment out of my head, about her partner having a long reach."

She opened the first drawer to his desk. There was nothing but a few paper clips and empty mint wrappers. Which Sienna concluded, were used to cover the smell of alcohol on the former DCI's breath. Opening the second drawer, she paused and looked at Callum. He walked over to see what she had found.

"Shit!" he exclaimed. He reached down and picked up the contents of the drawer. He held up a roll of sandwich bags. He turned to Joyce. "What was Doyle's behaviour like after PC Markowska left?"

Moving her eyes to the side, recalling the event, she answered slowly, realising the relevance of the contents of the drawer and subsequent question. "He was like a bear with a sore head. I assumed it was because he might have learned he was being investigated."

"Does Doyle have any family to speak of?"

"Yes, a sister." Joyce turned and headed out the door, "I'll have an officer bring her in first thing in the morning."

Chapter 37

Demolition vehicles had arrived on Acer Avenue, ready to tear down the derelict buildings. Ron, the foreman, and his labourers were making a final walk through the factories.

There had been an uptake in homeless people seeking sanctuary in the buildings recently. In fact, Ron thought there had been an uptake in homelessness everywhere lately. *Fucking government, they'll be charging us for air next. Poor fuckers are gonna have nowhere once this place is gone.*

The factories were to be demolished to make way for 'affordable housing.' *Affordable housing my arse, maybe if you're earning fifty grand a year and shagging the taxman,* he thought bitterly.

He saw an abandoned red car with the driver's side door open. *Shit, I'll have to get the old bill down here now, poxy kids, should be at home, playing with their dicks, not out nicking cars,* he thought, lifting his hard hat to scratch his head.

He finished the sweep of the first building and walked on to the next, pulling back the already lose shuttering. *Poor buggers have been in here alright.* He thought, feeling terrible that he'd have to be the one to turf them out. Leaning the shuttering to one side, he stepped into the building and looked up at the old scaffold tower in the middle of the now empty factory floor. *Fuck me!* He stepped back hitting the wall behind him, emitting a cloud of dust, from the old brickwork.

Fighting to keep down his breakfast, he ran to the first labourer he saw. "Get the fucking old bill down here now!" He demanded. "What's up?" The labourer ran in his direction, wondering what all the commotion was about. Ron, who was now clutching his chest, could say nothing. He bent over, his arm outstretched, pointing to the factory. The Labourer went in, looked up, and quickly wished he hadn't.

When DCI Sloane arrived half an hour later, the foreman had been taken away in an ambulance. He had a massive heart attack and it was touch and go if he would make it.

The DCI walked into the factory with DI Khatri to see PC Claire Mitchell, suspended on the scaffold tower with her arms and legs spread out wide. She was naked, covered in deep lacerations, arranged in a symmetrical pattern. Attached to her bloodied left breast, with a screwdriver, was a photo of Sienna looking in a shop window. When she was finally cut down, they found a screwed-up ball of paper stuffed into her mouth. The crime scene officer photographed, then removed the note, placed it in an evidence bag and passed it to the DCI who read it out to DI Khatri.

Dear Dr Turner,

Sorry, I became distracted from coming to you next.

However, you took what's mine, so I took one of yours.

Who's superior now?

You won't see me coming.

Chapter 38

Sienna sat with Joyce in the interview room opposite the large woman with bleached blonde hair. The sister of former DCI George Doyle was looking quite perturbed but not altogether surprised that she had been asked to come in and answer some questions about her brother.

"So, come on then, what's he done? I mean, I assume that's why you want to ask me about him. So, what is it?"

Without answering the question, Joyce was the first to respond, "What can you tell me about your brother's relationships with women?"

"There wasn't any, at least not since the last time I saw him, over a month ago, when he moved away."

"And before that?" Joyce encouraged.

"He was seeing someone from work for, about six months or so."

"What happened?"

"She left him," she folded her arms, looking indignant, "not that I blame the poor sap."

"He wasn't very nice to her then." Sienna confirmed.

"You lot know him. He wasn't very nice to anyone." she looked down to the floor, "Never was."

"Can you elaborate." Sienna urged.

"Well he beat his first wife to a pulp, not that you lot did anything." She indicated towards the two in front of her, but it was clear she was referring to the police force in general.

"How long ago was that?"

"What d'ya mean how long ago? He beat her for over ten years until the poor cow built up the courage to get out of there. They couldn't have kids. It was down to him, low sperm count." She sneered as she spoke "Not that it stopped him blaming her for it of course. Poor cow. I even helped her. Gave her some money, to get herself sorted."

"Do you know where she is now?"

"Nope! Never heard from her again, didn't expect to either."

"So, when did Mrs Doyle leave?" Sienna queried.

"Bout eight months ago, I suppose. George went off his head. I never told him I helped her and I don't want you lot telling him." She suddenly looked worried about the information she was providing.

Joyce leant forward, "I promise you, anything you say in this room is between us." She reassured.

Relaxing, Doyle's sister began again. "He was always a pig. He killed my puppy once when we were kids. Told me it was an accident but it wasn't. It was because he wasn't allowed one."

Sienna leant on the table with her forearms. "Do you mind me asking what your home life was like when you were children?"

Dropping her eyes to the floor again, shifting in her seat, she answered. "Hell, is one way to describe it I s'pose." She sat up straighter now and relayed the background of Doyle's childhood.

George Doyle was the youngest of three children. All three of them had been regularly sexually abused and beaten by their father who was a dock worker in Southampton. Their mother, who was an alcoholic, did nothing to protect any of them. The father eventually ended up in prison after he had murdered their mother, stabbing her sixteen times with a vegetable knife before cutting her throat.

The children spent the remainder of their childhood being moved from one children's home to another. In the final home George lived in, he was raped, by a male member of staff. He tried to report it to a female member of staff, but he was punished for telling lies. After that, George was fostered out separately from his siblings, where he stayed until he joined the police force.

Doyle's sister, finished her story and Sienna placed her hand over hers. "I am so sorry you had to go through all that. I understand how difficult to relive it all."

"Do you? I mean do you really?"

Sienna did not reply. She wished she could tell her that she understood perfectly what it was like to live through hell and come out the other side, just to go back through it again, but she couldn't.

Joyce broke the silence. "You say your brother moved away. Do you know where he went?"

"No and I don't want to know." She sniffed. "All I know is he moved towards London way."

Wrapping up the interview, Joyce thanked Doyle's sister for coming in and went off to arrange for an officer to take her back home.

Sienna went out to Callum who had been listening to the interview.

"It's him, it has to be." She exclaimed.

"Without a doubt, Doc," He placed a hand on her cheek, she nestled against it lovingly. "I think we should go straight back to Highbridge, there's not much more for us here."

"I agree. I'll go and speak to Joyce and get a copy of the interview etcetera, can you ring Terry and update him."

Kissing her forehead, he winked at her. "I'll be right back."

Sienna said her goodbyes to Joyce, and armed with all the new evidence they had collected, she walked outside into the sunshine. Callum was leaning up against his car. As she got closer, she could see he was looking troubled.

"What's the matter, Cal? What's happened?"

Callum placing his hands supportively on Sienna's arms. "There's been another murder."

Sienna stared at him blankly, "We need to get back now." She went to pull away to get in the car but Callum held on to her.

"Si, listen." He was speaking softly and Sienna's heart was in her mouth. Callum continued, "The victim's Claire Mitchell."

Sienna opened her mouth to speak and closed it again. She looked around her, not knowing why, before looking back up at Callum. "No!" she exclaimed, "Are they sure?"

Callum confirmed it was definitely Claire and filled her in on everything he had been told, including the note that had been left for her. The anger was surging through Sienna like a hurricane. She thought of the lovely probationary officer who did not have a bad word to say about anybody. A young woman, just starting out in life, excited and full of hopes for the future, had just had her life snuffed out. Targeted because of the hate Doyle had for Sienna.

Pulling herself together, she looked back up at Callum, her eyes were wild with rage. "We need to get this bastard."

Callum pulled her to him, holding her until she was calm. "We will Si, I promise."

Chapter 39

The crime scene officers had combed Cheryl Markowska's house thoroughly. DNA found both surrounding and on the kitchen table had been matched to Emilie Wythe. DNA was also matched to, Cheryl Markowska and an unknown male.

Cheryl's computer had been seized. On it was a link to the chat room account, which was set up with a fake profile and photographs of Emilie Wythe, Elaine Jackson, and finally Sienna. These were mainly chance pictures of Sienna shopping, entering her apartment, or getting into her car. As random as they were, they were doubly worrying for all involved in the case.

PC Mitchell's mother had been informed of her death, and by the time Sienna and Callum had arrived back at Highbridge, the front of the station was already being lined with flowers and candles from well-meaning members of the public.

As they drove towards the station's gates, press and photographers, surrounded the vehicle, before being pushed back by officers, allowing the couple to pass through. The DCI was at the back entrance to meet them. He looked dishevelled and exhausted, having spent the night at the station going over statements and trying to get more information from Cheryl Markowska.

Giving the pair only half a chance to get out of the car, the DCI clapped his hands together, "Pleased to see you both made it back ok, but we need to get on."

Walking sideways as he spoke to them, he added in a louder than usual voice, "I'm sick of this arrogant bastard, thinking he can get away with killing one of my officers and threaten my colleagues," he spoke quieter now adding, "people I care about."

The DCI's affection for Sienna, was apparent to everyone, and Sienna's heart went out to him as she could see he was struggling to deal with the latest killing and subsequent threat to her.

Bellowing over his shoulder as he walked away, "Get yourselves sorted then meet me upstairs. I want a full update right away." The DCI pushed through the doors and stormed off, towards the stairs.

"Think it's going to be a long day." Callum remarked, looking down at Sienna, putting his arm round her as they walked into the station together.

Inside of the station was eerily quiet, even though there were more officers on duty than usual. Many of them had volunteered for double duty. Desperate to avenge the death of their colleague. With one fellow officer arrested for murder, and one murdered, morale was at an all-time low.

Dave Fletcher was in the custody suite when they arrived and greeted them both, shaking Callum's hand and pulling Sienna in for a sisterly hug. "Glad you got back okay."

Wanting to get to the point, Dave continued, "Cal mate, I know you've just got back, but we need to speak to the troops. The Chief Inspectors off, so it's down to us to get this lot boosted."

"No problem, mate. I just need to update the DCI."

"It's okay, you do what you need to do down here, I'll update the DCI." She offered as she took the bag containing the interview tapes and sandwich bags from Callum. He thanked her and bent to kiss her.

"Well it's about fucking time." Dave snorted. "I take it the eagle not only landed but built a nest." He mocked, winking at Sienna as he spoke.

"Fuck off, Dave." Callum laughed, looking at Sienna apologetically.

"On that note, I'm going to leave the nursery and head on upstairs to big school." Excusing herself, she added "Ladies!" She winked at Callum, who was relieved she wasn't offended and walked off.

Dave stood with Callum and watched her walk away, before rapping Callum lightly on his chest with the back off his hand. "You, jammy bastard." He jeered.

Callum put him in a head lock and proceeded to rub his head with his knuckles, "Fuck off, Dave." He laughed.

Chapter 40

Sienna walked into the DCI's office to see him sitting at his desk with his head on his hands.

"I take it you haven't slept Terry?"

Looking up, he smiled weakly, "Doc, I'm sorry for barking at you. I'm just fed up with this maniac running rings around us."

"I get it Terry, we will get him. If it's the last thing I ever do, we'll get him." She spoke with conviction but she hoped, it would be before anyone else died.

"So, fill me in on Doyle."

Sienna sat down and explained at length, the details of Doyle's dismissal, his sister's account of his life, the abuse he subjected his ex-wife to, the fact he had a girlfriend who was believed to be a police officer from Dorset. She showed him the evidence bag containing the roll of sandwich bags.

They went into the incident room with the rest of the investigation team and listened to the statement from Doyle's sister.

The DCI walked to the centre of the room. "Well, he certainly looks good for it but we need more than his sister's statement and a roll of bags." He rubbed his furrowed brow, circling the space at the front of the room.

Baz offered his thoughts on the matter, "We've got enough to bring him in Guv, plus we have the unknown DNA sample. We just need to match that to Doyle."

"True," The DCI agreed, "but we need to find Doyle first plus the DNA only puts him at the scene."

"Doc, can you speak to Markowska again? Speak to her about Doyle, see how she reacts." Turning to DI Khatri, he continued. "Baz, can you find an address for Doyle, see where he's been staying or working."

"DCI Pembury told me he got quite a nice 'retirement package', so there's a chance he won't be working." Sienna interjected.

Nodding the DCI replied, "Even so, there's gotta be a paper trail somewhere. Baz check everything, bank, credit cards the lot. I want to know where and when he last had a shit and where he's gonna have the next one."

DI Khatri walked towards the door. "I'll get on to it now."

Grateful for the new information and a possible direction to go in, the DCI turned back to Sienna. "Where's Cal."

"Downstairs briefing room with Sergeant Fletcher rallying the troops. Dave, felt they could do with a bit of a morale boost." She smiled before adding "I think Cal would be better suited doing that than Dave, you know how he likes to put things."

The DCI laughed, "Yeah, he's not the subtlest of men. He's a goodun though."

Sienna agreed, despite his brash way of putting things, it was difficult not to like him. Plus, she was grateful to him for helping Callum get his head straight.

Looking more thoughtful now, the DCI asked, "So," he started cautiously, "am I allowed to ask if you two kids are okay?"

Sienna blushed a little, "Yes, Terry. Us 'kids' are more than okay."

The DCI beamed, "Best news I've heard in ages." He hugged Sienna tight.

"Right," he boomed, clapping his hands together, "back to business, shall we go and speak to Markowska?"

"Lead the way, Dad." She smirked, warmly.

Cheryl looked a lot calmer than the last time Sienna had seen her. She also looked exhausted. Her eyes were red and swollen from crying and her hair was badly tangled.

"Have you managed to eat or sleep at all Cheryl?" Sienna enquired fondly.

"A little I guess, thank you." She looked down and took a deep breath.

"I... I'm sorry to hear about Claire. I didn't know he was going to do that."

The DCI responded, "If you did know, would you have done anything about it?"

"I wish I could say that I would, Claire was nice."

"They were all nice, Cheryl!" The DCI was already getting frustrated. Sienna could understand his agitation, and if she was honest, she wanted to scream at Cheryl herself, but it would get them nowhere.

Interrupting the DCI, she addressed Cheryl herself, "Cheryl, I'd like to take you back to Dorset if I may. Did you have a close friend or boyfriend while you were there?"

Cheryl put her head down.

"Cheryl, don't look at the floor, look at me. Your friend has been murdered and he is coming after me. Is that what you want?"

"No, of course not but,"

"No buts, Cheryl. Answer my question, it's a simple one. Did you have a boyfriend in Dorset?"

"Yes."

"Thank you. Now, did you work with DCI George Doyle, when you was at Dorset."

Cheryl's head shot to the floor, the DCI and Sienna could see her physically shake. Sienna, and the DCI looked at each other before the DCI spoke to Cheryl again. "Cheryl, I'm going to ask you something, but before I do I need you to know, nobody, and I mean nobody can get to you at this station. I promise you that. Now, do you believe me?"

Cheryl, didn't answer for a while. Then she lifted her head, "I believe you."

"Good, now Cheryl, was you having a relationship with DCI Doyle?"

Looking down again, she nodded.

Sienna prompted her to speak. "Cheryl, we need to hear you say it out loud."

"Yes," she replied shakily, "yes I was having a relationship with DCI Doyle."

"Thank you, Cheryl. Now can you tell me if DCI Doyle is living in Highbridge?"

"No. he's staying with me." She explained, shaking her head.

Sienna looked again to the DCI, both confused, the DCI went on "As you know, we've been to your house, and secured evidence from there. Doyle wasn't there."

"No, not in Highbridge." She looked equally perturbed now. "Sorry, I thought you knew by now. That wasn't where I was living. I had to rent that out for," Cheryl stopped in her tracks.

"I have a place in Wendon. It was my mother's house, it's still in her name." She paused, "Maybe that's why you didn't find out about it." She offered, more quietly now.

"Cheryl, now remember what I told you. You are safe here okay?" The DCI reiterated.

Cheryl indicated her agreement again.

The DCI leaned forward so he was looking at Cheryl directly, "Did former DCI George Doyle, murder Emile Wythe and Elaine Jackson?"

Cheryl put her head down as she nodded and began to cry.

Cheryl, I need you to speak for the tape. "Did Former DCI George Doyle murder Emilie Wythe and Elaine Jackson?"

"Yes!" As she spoke, she broke down, her shoulders slumped, partly from relief, partly from exhaustion. Heaving cries left her body.

They sat with her quietly until she was calm enough to speak again.

Sienna covered her hands, "Cheryl, can you give us your address in Wendon and anything you can tell us about his routine?"

"Yes," she confirmed, finally relieved to have the whole horrific nightmare out in the open. "I'll tell you anything you need to know. I'll even tell you where he put his ex-wife."

Chapter 41

For the rest of the interview, Cheryl sung like the proverbial bird. She supplied her address in Wendon, describing the property in detail. Told them about the DVD's he had made, not only of the killings in Highbridge, but also the murder of his ex-wife, and Woodland murders in Dorset.

She told them about their relationship, how he was the perfect gentleman at first, buying her gifts and showering her with affection. The first time he had hit her and the first time he had raped her.

She relayed how he had injected her into the murders of Emilie Wythe and Elaine Jackson, forced her to watch, while he tortured and murdered them before raping her while she was in the same room as the dead bodies.

Cheryl went on to reel off a list dates, times, and places that they had been even the name of the pub Doyle liked to frequent. She recalled everything she had bottled up for so long as is if she was reading it from a script.

By the time they had finished, they had everything they needed to arrest Doyle. The only thing they didn't have was Doyle himself.

----o----

The briefing room was filled to bursting point with both CID and uniformed officers. The DCI, DI Khatri, Callum, and Sienna stood at the front of the room, relaying everything they had learned over the last thirty-six hours.

Morale was rising back to the top at lightning speed as the officers of Highbridge learned that they were inches away from bringing in the murderer of their colleague.

The team was arranged in groups to attend all the addresses Cheryl had supplied them with and everyone was ready to go. The DCI and DI Khatri planned to go to the address in Wendon.

"Cal, I know you deserve to be at the arrest, but I want you and Sienna to go home. Make sure she's safe, I'll have an officer posted back outside your property." Sienna was about to protest but was firmly put in her place by the fatherly DCI.

"For once in your life Doc, you'll do as your bloody told. Besides, you two have been working non-stop for 36 hours. You're no good to me out there."

Sienna thought he was a fine one to talk, having been at work the same hours as her, but even Sienna knew when she was beat. Plus, if she was honest, she was beyond exhausted.

"Okay, but as long as you promise to keep us updated." She reasoned.

"Wouldn't have it any other way, Doc." Now go on, we'll have Doyle in custody within the next hour or so."

Callum put his arm round Sienna, "Come on trouble, let's get you out of here before you get other ideas."

He looked towards the DCI, "Good luck, Guv." As he led Sienna downstairs and out of the building.

Chapter 42

Callum had stopped at his apartment to pick up a change of clothes. Sienna wanted to go up to her place to get a shower. She insisted she would be fine as there was an officer outside and she was only upstairs. She gave Callum her spare key to let himself in. After a long, lingering kiss he told her to keep the shower running for him.

Rushing to throw clean clothes in his bag, he couldn't wait to get upstairs. The thought of joining Sienna in the shower again was rendering him useless as he struggled to zip up the bag. Laughing to himself over the way she could make him so flustered, he headed for the door. His mobile rang, it was Dominic. Not wanting to miss his call, he dropped the bag down, and answered the call.

The PC who sat in his car outside Sienna's apartment, was a little disappointed that he wasn't with his colleagues, bringing in Doyle. Wanting to be where the action was, he couldn't believe his bad luck when he was assigned to baby-sitting duties. He was also desperate to go to the toilet and cursed himself for not going before he left the station.

Getting out of the car, he looked around to see if anyone was watching. With no body, around, he decided to risk going to the bushes near the apartment so he could relieve himself. Shadowing himself in the bushes as much as possible, he undone his fly and rolled his eyes in relief as he emptied his bladder into the bush. As he did up his fly, he heard a noise to the left of him.

Walking over to where the noise was coming from, he heard it again. *It's coming from the bin store*, he thought as he felt for his torch, while extending his baton ready to strike. Standing sideways with his baton raised he swung open the door. A loud crash emitted from the back of the bin store. Before the PC could react, a cat jumped out at him. The cat, who was just as frightened as the officer, hissed in the officer's face before springing from his chest and fleeing in the opposite direction. *Fucking hate cats* he thought to himself as he turned to shine the torch back in the bin store. He didn't hear Doyle behind him as he was about to close the door. He also didn't see Doyle, as he struck him on the back of the head, knocking him unconscious before pushing him into the bin store and closing the door.

Walking over to the main entrance, Doyle buzzed on a random door number. Explaining to the occupant he lived at number eleven, and had forgotten his key, he smiled to himself as he was let into the building. *Will these people never learn about security*, he grinned as he walked up the stairs.

Sienna got two wine glasses down from the cupboard and opened a bottle of wine to let it breathe. She headed towards the bedroom to get undressed when there was a knock at the door. *He's forgotten I gave him a key already,* she thought as she headed to the door.

"Your brain is like a sieve." She called out amused, and pulled open the door.

She stepped back in terror, as she saw Doyle stood before her. She tried to push the door shut but he was too fast. Pushing his way through, he kicked the door closed behind him and began walking towards her slowly.

"I shoulda sorted you in Dorset, you interfering slut." He snarled. "But don't fret, that's a mistake I'm gonna correct."

Sienna shook from head to toe. Fear coursing through her veins. She walked backwards slowly, towards the kitchen, edging her way round the counter.

"Callum will be here any minute." Her voice cracked as she spoke.

"Your boyfriend's busy." he hissed. "No one helps dirty interfering whores." He tilted his head to one side, looking at her jeeringly. "You shoulda realised that by now."

By now she was trapped. Her back was up against the fridge. He grabbed her by the throat and squeezed. She could feel his fingers pushing into her larynx.

"I wonder what he'll do when he finds his dirty little whore, gutted like a fish. I can just see him now, picking up bits and pieces of you, crying like a bitch."

He snarled in her face, his bitter acrid breath made the bile churn in her stomach. He was crushing her throat, her ears started to ring. She stretched out her arm to the sideboard next to her, searching, for anything.

Her hand made contact, with the coffee pot. She brought it up, smashing it into the side of his head. He reeled sideways releasing his grip from her throat. Sienna darted to the side and ran for the door. Panicking she struggled to open it.

He was there behind her. Grabbing her by the hair, he pulled her back with such force, she landed hard on her back, banging her head on the floor as she went down. She tried to get up, but he was in top of her. His face was in hers, as she breathed in the foul dampness of his skin.

"I'm gonna show you what a real man feels like, before I slit you, open and pull out your guts." He spat. "I've never fucked a brunette, or a shrink before, but there's always a first time."

His vile words gave Sienna a new-found power. Freeing her hand, she forced her thumb in his eye. He screamed in pain, clutching his eye as, blood ran through his fingers.

"You'll have to kill me first." She managed to scream, trying her hardest to struggle free from under him, but he was too strong. "Have it your way." He slapped her round the face so forcefully, Sienna's head snapped back onto the floor, causing her head to spin.

Subdued, he grabbed her wrists and pinned them above her head with one hand. His grip was vice like and she couldn't get free. The other hand was back round her throat and he was squeezing again.

His blood was dripping on to her face and, she felt the bile rise up from her stomach.

"You're gonna fucking pay for that you little fucking bitch!" He was screaming at her now, spraying saliva as he hurled abuse at her.

She brought her knee up hard into his crotch causing him to double up. Doyle screamed out in pain and rolled off her grabbing his groin. Sienna rolled over, and crawled on her hands and knees to get away from him. He grabbed her ankles and pulled her back.

She could feel her strength waning. He flipped her over and straddled her, pinning her arms to her sides with his knees, sitting on her with his full weight. He raised his hand and brought it down, hitting her hard across the jaw with the back of his hand. Searing pain shot through her head like a bullet as her cheek split open. She could feel the warmth of her blood spill down her cheek, into her ear, and she saw the room going dark as she fought to stay conscious.

"You fucking whore, you think you're so fucking superior, you think you're better than me, you think you can beat me? Well, who's beating who now you, dirty little slut!" Doyle reached into his jacket pocket and pulled out a small vegetable knife.

He raised his free hand to hit her again. Sienna knew she was going to die. She thought of Lilly and Jack and never seeing them again. Then she thought of Callum. She could see him in her mind. Believing he was the last thing she'd see, she felt strangely calm.

Still screaming obscenities at her, Doyle brought his hand down towards her. Hitting her again, blood sprayed from her mouth and she bit her own tongue as he made contact. He dug the tip of the knife into her shoulder. "Just for your boyfriend, I'm gonna design a whole new pattern." He pushed the knife into her shoulder, until the blade went in right up to the hilt and Sienna shut her eyes tightly, fighting off the pain, refusing to scream, refusing to give him the fear he craved. Her blood spilled out, pooling on the floor around her.

Doyle laughed as he pulled the blade out, causing the flow of blood to increase. "Trust me bitch, you will scream by the time I've finished with you, you'll be begging me for death." He was bellowing at her as he gripped either side of her blouse and ripped it open, exposing her bra.

"In your dreams you bastard…" Sienna barely managed to mutter. Doyle hit her again. Sienna knew her time would soon be up, as she fought with every breath to stay alive.

"Let's go here next." He sang loudly, as he pointed the tip of the knife in the flesh of her right breast.

Callum was finishing his call to Dominic, as he got into the lift. "I'll video call you at the weekend mate, there's someone I want you to meet."

The lift door opened as he hung up the call.

He could hear shouting, and it took a second or two to register it was coming from Sienna's apartment. *Doyle!* He thought in panic. He dropped his bag in the doorway of the lift and sprinted to her door.

Stopping at the door, Callum listened briefly, trying to assess the situation. His heart was thundering in his ears, adrenaline flooding his body. Sienna was in serious trouble.

He burst through the door, kicking it off his hinges. He grabbed Doyle, yanking him off Sienna. Doyle fell onto his side, the knife, slipped from his grasp and slid across the floor out of reach. Callum swung his leg forward, kicking him with full force in the stomach. Doyle doubled over in agony, vomiting bile from the force of the kick.

Callum was beyond anger now as he was taken over by rage. He was on Doyle in a split second. He brought his fist down, punching him hard on the side of the head, instantly knocking him out cold. The red mist of Callum's rage, wasn't abating, and he hit Doyle again.

Sienna was barely conscious herself, but she knew she had to stop Callum from killing him. She managed to stretch out her hand, reaching his arm, she could barely speak.

"Cal, stop." She croaked. Her larynx was badly bruised and she could barely make her words audible.

Remembering her promise to him, she tried again. "Cal, please, I need you."

It was enough to catch his attention. With Doyle unconscious, Callum crawled off him, and went to Sienna.

"Oh, god Si, what has he done to you?" He gently lifted her to a sitting position, and cradled her in his arms. He tore a length off her already ripped blouse, and pushed it down on to her shoulder wound, holding it firmly in place to stem the flow of blood. She winced in pain. "I'm sorry, baby. I have to do this."

A cold darkness filled Sienna's mind as, she slipped into unconsciousness. Callum pulled out his phone and dialled for an ambulance.

He sat there gently rocking her in his arms, tears cascaded down his cheeks. "Stay with me baby, stay with me." He sobbed.

Chapter 43

Checking his appearance in the mirror, Callum, brushed off the shoulder of his smart black tailored suit. It was important to look his best today.

It had been fourteen days since the arrest of George Doyle, who was now blind in one eye and had to have twelve stitches to his face. They had enough evidence to formerly charge him with all the murders, and he would be going away for a very long time. Cheryl Markowska, would also serve time in prison. However, due to mitigating circumstances, she was likely to get a lesser sentence.

Checking himself over for a final time, he picked up a large spray of deep red roses, *the same colour as the dress, Sienna wore to the charity ball*, he remembered fondly, blinking back tears as he headed out the door.

Arriving at the station, he walked into the custody suite. Officers stopped to watch him as he walked along the corridor, past the sergeant's office, to Sienna's door. He leant up against the door frame, looking into the room.

Looking up from her desk, Sienna smiled warmly. She had returned to work within a week of Doyle's arrest, much to the protests of both Callum, and the DCI. However, she was insistent she needed to make sure all her reports were accurate and up to date ready for Doyle's trial. After the fight she had put up with Doyle, neither of them were about to argue.

Her bruising had now faded. However, she was going to be left with a permanent half inch scar on her cheekbone. The wound on her shoulder was healing nicely, and she was finally able to get rid of the sling she had to begrudgingly wear. She would still need physiotherapy on her arm and shoulder to get the full movement back. She had to have an MRI to check for swelling on her brain, but she had been given the all clear, and was well on the road to a full recovery. Externally at least.

Callum couldn't help but wonder, how many internal scars this amazing woman could take before she finally broke completely. He swore to himself, and to her, that she would never hurt again as long as he lived.

Sienna got up from her desk and walked over to Callum. He swept her up with one arm, kissing her passionately. Putting her down gently, he handed her the spray of roses.

Taking the flowers from him, she eyed him in mock suspicion. "Okay, what have you done?"

"Hey! Can't I get my woman flowers without me doing anything wrong?" He joked.

"Probably not!" she exclaimed, "And since when, did I become your 'woman' captain caveman?"

Laughing, Callum argued, "I'm never gonna bloody win with you, am I?"

Sienna kissed him, "Once again, Sergeant Blake, you are correct." She teased playfully, "There's hope for you yet."

"You're a real piece of work, do you know that?" He grinned. "Oh, and for your information," he pulled her tight into his arms, "You became my woman, from the first moment, I spoke to you. I love you Dr Turner. Always have, always will."

Placing the flowers on the desk, she laced her fingers around his neck, wincing slightly as she raised her arm. "That's one thing, I won't argue with. Oh, and for the record Sergeant Blake," her face softened, she gazed into his piercing blue eyes hoping she would drown in them, "I love you too, more than life itself."

Breaking the spell briefly, Sienna asked, "Now, what times your interview?"

The expansion to the Serious Crime Unit had been approved and Callum had been recommended for promotion. The interview was just a formality to transfer over to the new unit. Sienna had also accepted the offer of working with them. Although she insisted on still lecturing at universities.

"We've got half an hour," raising his eyebrows suggestively. "Now read the card in your flowers while I decide what I'm going to do with you." He winked.

Sienna reached for the card and pulled it from the small envelope. She smiled widely as, she read.

I've finally found the perfect menu.

I love you, Si. Always and forever xxx

They kissed as if they were the only people left in the world. The love they had for each other, pushing them closer. In the space of two months, they had found each other, and Callum had already nearly lost her to the hands of George Doyle. Fourteen days ago, he had held her limp, almost lifeless body in his arms. Thinking she had been taken from him, in that moment, he did not want to live. He loved her ferociously with every cell in his body. She had consumed him, mind, body, and soul.

Sienna learned not only that true love was possible, but that it was wonderful. She had learned what it was to love, to want and to need someone. She didn't want to even imagine a life without Callum in it. So strong was her love for him, she found it hard to breathe when he wasn't there.

She had battled through life and had been left with many scars, but, with Callum's love, she had learned, the scars couldn't decide her future, they were merely symbols of her past that drove her forward. The direction she chose to go in, was up to her and she loved the path she was on.

----o----

Printed in Great Britain
by Amazon